"Couldn't find a larger towel?" Shea asked, motioning Duke into the tub.

"It'd be like putting a raincoat on a Greek statue," he teased.

She watched, hypnotized despite herself, as he eased down into the mud. His back muscles rippled in a symphony of male perfection, his bronzed body made her want—

"Oink," he said gruffly.

She chuckled and poured the buckets of mud over his legs and torso.

"Now what?" he asked.

"Now you lie back, close your eyes, and I'll massage your scalp."

He rested his head on a pillow and did as she said. Shea smiled, then dumped her last bucket of mud onto his head.

Duke sat up, sputtered, then grabbed for her with both hands. "Take a wallow with me, hellion!"

"Please, no," she yelped, one second before he pulled her into the tub.

She began laughing helplessly as she sank into the mud between his knees. He shook his head, slinging mud everywhere. "You play hard, *querida*. I like that," he said in a voice that was half angry, half amused. "But you've toyed with a master gamesman. You've thrown down a challenge. . . ."

"Quiet, *hombre*," Shea said, and kissed him.

He went still for a moment, then wrapped his arms around her possessively. Twisting his mouth against hers, the kiss went from giddy to wild to wanton. . . .

WHAT ARE *LOVESWEPT* ROMANCES?

They are stories of true romance and touching emotion. We believe those two very important ingredients are constants in our highly sensual and very believable stories in the *LOVESWEPT* line. Our goal is to give you, the reader, stories of consistently high quality that may sometimes make you laugh, sometimes make you cry, but are always fresh and creative and contain many delightful surprises within their pages.

Most romance fans read an enormous number of books. Those they truly love, they keep. Others may be traded with friends and soon forgotten. We hope that each *LOVESWEPT* romance will be a treasure—a "keeper." We will always try to publish

LOVE STORIES YOU'LL NEVER FORGET
BY AUTHORS YOU'LL ALWAYS REMEMBER

The Editors

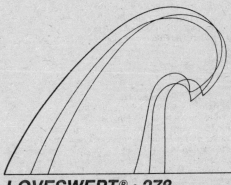

LOVESWEPT® · 278

Deborah Smith
California Royale

 BANTAM BOOKS
TORONTO · NEW YORK · LONDON · SYDNEY · AUCKLAND

CALIFORNIA ROYALE

A Bantam Book / September 1988

*LOVESWEPT® and the wave device are registered
trademarks of Bantam Books, a division of
Bantam Doubleday Dell Publishing Group, Inc.
Registered in U.S. Patent
and Trademark Office and elsewhere.*

*If you would be interested in receiving protective vinyl
covers for your Loveswept books, please write to this address
for information:*

*Loveswept
Bantam Books
P.O. Box 985
Hicksville, NY 11802*

ISBN 0-553-21918-9

Published simultaneously in the United States and Canada

*Bantam Books are published by Bantam Books, a division
of Bantam Doubleday Dell Publishing Group, Inc. Its trademark, consisting of the words "Bantam Books" and the
portrayal of a rooster, is Registered in U.S. Patent and
Trademark Office and in other countries. Marca Registrada.
Bantam Books, 666 Fifth Avenue, New York, New York 10103.*

PRINTED IN THE UNITED STATES OF AMERICA

O   0 9 8 7 6 5 4 3 2 1

*To the Young Women's Luncheon Club,
a lovely and very eccentric group of ladies
who believe in sisterhood, good times,
and white gloves.*

One

The last thing Duke Araiza needed was a fat farm.

Estate Mendocino was precisely that, he thought ruefully as he ambled down a corridor decorated with Italian tile, expensive art deco lamps, and oriental rugs. The huge resort embodied frivolous luxury from the tip of its French chateau turrets to the manicured greens of its golf course.

It was late evening. The rich and famous were all in their silk-sheeted beds, he assumed. Duke whistled in his typically nonchalant way as he strolled down the elegant hallway until he came to a door with a placard that read, Mud Therapy and Massage—Women. He hesitated for only a moment, then pushed the door open. He walked through a dimly lit changing room, frowning at the solid-oak lockers and the crystal dispensers full of mineral water.

Ornately carved doors—all shut—lined both sides of the room. But at the end of the hallway one door stood open, and the light poured out. Duke ran a hand through hair as black as a winter night, cleared his throat, and strolled through the doorway.

A woman reclined in a claw-footed tub full of stuff that looked like a chocolate pudding with a bad identity problem. Duke stopped, amazed at the sight of her. Her beautiful small breasts were revealed above the mire that hid the rest of her body.

"So this is mud therapy," Duke said under his breath. "I could get to like it."

Her head was tilted back on the rim of the tub, and her eyes were closed. She had draped her slender, slightly muscular arms along either side of the tub. The cinnamon polish on her perfectly manicured nails coordinated with the room's pink-and-brown color scheme. Everything about her whispered class.

Duke watched the light of a single wall lamp weave golden tones through the wavy hair that flowed over the tub's edge. That hair he thought, had to match the color of the Spanish gold piece he carried in his pocket. Duke moved quietly to the side of the tub and gazed down at her, fascinated. He could smell her perfume, unobscurred by the damp-clay smell of mud. Roses and cream, old-fashioned and delicate.

Shea Somerton believed in psychic powers, but she was too practical to think that she might have them herself. Now, however, she felt the strangest urge to open her eyes. It was as if a key had been turned somewhere deep in her soul, driving away the restful blankness she had sought after a long day's work. She raised her head languidly and let her eyelids flutter open.

The first things she saw were snugly blue-jeaned thighs below a muscular, broad chest outlined in a clingy white pullover. In the instant of shock that followed, her gaze rose to an angular, richly tanned face with eyes as dark as burnt wood.

Thick black hair was tossled over that face, a strand or two wisping forward to grace an intelligent brow wrinkled in concentration. A heart-stopping man looked down at her with a slightly chagrined smile—he knew he was someplace he should not be—but his eyes crinkled with laughter.

"I never thought mud could look so good," he said jovially.

Shea gasped and sank lower in the tub. She was alone here, she realized. It was after ten and the staff was gone, and this exotic looking interloper was staring at her as if she were salsa and he the taco chip.

She composed herself and answered drolly, "The mud won't look so good if I plaster it over your eyes. *Scram.*" She paused, then added, "Please."

Duke's smile widened with admiration for her sass. The woman gazing up at him with a mixture of concern and bravado had a somewhat waifish face made unforgettable by a Sophia Loren mouth and turbulent violet eyes. Liz Taylor eyes, that's what they were. He'd never seen a face like this woman's.

"Sorry," he said with sincere apology. "I was just exploring, and I wanted to see what mud therapy involved." Duke rarely did anything he was told to do, so he didn't scram. Instead he retrieved a redwood-slat folding chair from its place by one wall of the small room and brought it close to the tub. He turned the chair around so that its back was toward the woman's wide, beautiful eyes, straddled it, and sat down.

"My name's Duke," he said politely.

"Your name is *mud* if you don't get out of here." Shea shook her head in exasperation at the inadvertent choice of words.

"Mud." He grinned. "Speaking of mud, what's that stuff like? What does it do for you?"

She tilted her head and looked at him with an icy, carefully composed smile. "Sir, are you a guest here?"

"Oh, yes, *ma'am.* I've got money and I'm fully certified." He reached in a back pocket of his jeans and produced a guest card. Shea caught only the flicker of green and gold—Estate Mendocino's colors—but it was enough to tell her that he was legitimate.

"Duke," she said in her most pleasant management voice, "this area is off-limits to male guests. The men's mud-therapy room closes at eight o'clock. Weren't you given instructions when you arrived?"

"Gonna have me tossed out? I wouldn't blame you."

"I don't believe *tossing* is necessary. But you really *should* leave."

He gazed at her with a warmth that would fire wet kindling. Now that she could think about something besides the racing of her heart, she noticed that his nose was straight, but had just the slightest hook to it. A fine white scar ran horizontally across the bridge, giving him a tough-guy appearance.

Shea was surprised that she found the look appealing rather than sinister. In her world of pampered and coiffed men, this man was unique. With such black hair and gleaming olive skin, he had to be of Spanish or Mexican background.

"I just got in a couple of hours ago," he explained. "I was supposed to drive up earlier, but I had a business meeting. I'll take the official tour in the morning." One large hand rose in a gesture that included not only the mud-bath room but the whole estate. "I want to see all of cotton-candy land."

Shea frowned at his derogatory assessment of the resort. This man didn't have an ounce of flab on a body that must have been well over six feet tall. He was the picture of fitness, and he didn't look like he needed to relax. He looked as if he were never anything *but* relaxed. So what was he doing at Estate Mendocino, the hangout of the rich and famous, the flabby and stressed out?

"You don't sound very enthusiastic about being here,"

she told him, then paused, feeling her skin tingle with an odd mixture of fear and excitement. This definitely was not the mud's mineral properties at work. "And *I'm* not very enthusiastic about your being here." She indicated the mud-therapy room with a firm movement of her hand. "Really, sir, this is a private . . . how did you get into this part of the resort after hours? Were the doors to the spa area unlocked?"

"Calm down, *querida*," he said in a gentle, serious voice. He wasn't going to tell her that he'd picked the lock. It would only upset her more. He shook his head. "I'm not that kind of man."

"I beg your pardon?"

"The kind who wants to frighten you. Who would try to frighten you." His expression lost its sincerity and became suspiciously solemn. "I just want to know about mud."

Shea exhaled sharply. He looked like some sort of old-West maverick: rough and handsome, with an attitude that seemed both gallant and rakish. She could either get out of the tub and march out of the room, or she could make conversation. Shea imagined his midnight eyes watching her as she walked, muddy and naked, toward the door. She sighed.

"The mud is good for your skin," she explained as calmly as she could. "You sit in the mud for a little while, then you take a shower, then you sit in an herbal bath, then you shower again, then you have a massage. When you're finished, you feel fantastic."

"Or else you have a craving to oink and squeal."

One corner of her mouth turned up in an involuntary smile. "But it would be *relaxed* oinking and squealing." He laughed lightly, the sound so warm and pleasant that Shea's nerves began to loosen. "We should put you to work here," she told him in a desperate attempt to make conversation. "You have one of those laughs that

makes people feel good." His eyes gleamed at the compliment, and Shea felt warmth spread down her body.
Oh, Lord, was she going crazy? He was a *stranger*.

"You work here?" he asked.

"Yes. I'm the estate's manager."

He arched one thick black brow and analyzed that
information with a surprised, then pleased, look. Shea
heard a sound and peered over the edge of the tub. The
toe of his scuffed brown cowboy boot was idly tapping
a rhythm on the white tiles.

"I tap when I think," he told her.

"Fred Astaire made a career of that."

He laughed again. "So where's someone to give you a
massage tonight?"

"Stop thinking, Fred." She frowned, deciding as she
did that she ought not to be so intrigued about this
unsettling stranger. "I'm just here for the mud bath
and a shower."

"You like being dirty, then you like getting clean.
Querida, you're my kind of lady. Take a shower and
let's go to dinner."

After a stunned moment Shea muttered something
in fluent Spanish. She wished that he'd stop calling
her *querida*. It meant "dearest."

He nodded, smiling and subtlely inhaling. The scent
of roses and cream would never leave his thoughts
now. "I'm a fast-talking *hombre*, that's for sure. Where
did you learn such street lingo?"

"Los Angeles. My hometown."

"Ah." Duke gazed at her thoughtfully. Though she
was covered in mud, he surmised that she was an
elegant, well-educated woman. Her command of barrio
Spanish continued to puzzle him. "It's nice to meet
another California native," he told her. "There aren't
many of us left."

"What part?"

"All of me."

"What part of *California?*" she emphasized in a droll tone.

"Imperial Valley. Near the Mexican border. Ranch and farm country."

"Are you ranch or farm?"

"I'm hungry," he answered with an authoritative nod. He wasn't about to let this straight-talking princess get away so easily. "How about dinner?"

Shea rubbed muddy fingers on her suddenly tense temples. "I can't fraternize with the guests. It's a management rule."

"Ah, but you're the manager. You can change the rules."

She shook her head. "Owner's rule, not mine. But it's a good one. Besides, guests aren't supposed to eat dinner away from the estate." She stared at him for a moment, her thoughts turbulent. "You don't even know my name."

"That's why we should have dinner. To learn names."

"The name is Shea Somerton. That eliminates the need for dinner."

He smiled. "I like it. The name, not the refusal to eat with me." He got up and went to a huge brass baker's rack on one wall. He retrieved a monogrammed pink hand towel and brought it back to her. Before Shea could reach up, he bent forward and carefully wiped the dabs of mud off her face.

Shea's senses went on complete alert. His fingertips brushed her skin, setting off interesting tingles. She looked up at him and was nearly lost in the gaze of earthy appreciation he didn't try to hide. He smelled virile and outdoorsy, unadorned by cologne. It was a refreshing change from the expensive and loud scents the male guests used, and Shea found herself responding to this assertive visitor's clean, masculine scent.

"Thank you," she said blankly when he finished. He smiled at her, his eyes so intense that the smile seemed only a polite gesture meant to reassure her that she was safe. Just barely. He ran one forefinger down to her lips, brushed them lightly, and nodded at her.

Shea looked away and scooped up a handful of mud, which she smeared across her upper chest as she tried to think straight. She had never understood the kind of spontaneous sexual reaction that provoked strangers to make intimate advances. That was the stuff of racy movies and soap opera episodes, not real life—not her regimented life, at least. Men complimented her on her muscle tone; they didn't burn her up with inviting looks.

"Is this a hint?" he asked. Shea turned her gaze upward. He gestured toward her chest. "You want me to clean more mud off you?"

There was nothing to do but laugh, so she did. This was an incredible encounter and it was completely hopeless.

"Get cleaned up and let's drive over to town for dinner," he urged again. "Are you married?"

"No."

"I'm not married either. I'm a lot of fun, and—"

"You're here to eat nutritiously. Your room has a well-stocked refrigerator, I'm certain."

"I'm not in a room. I have one of the cottages." He sighed grandly and straddled the chair again. "I looked in the refrigerator. Ten kinds of juices, a hundred kinds of vegetables, flat, ugly crackers—you call that eating?"

Now it was Shea's turn to raise a brow. A week in one of the estate's regular rooms, including the fitness and health program, cost three thousand dollars. A week in one of the cottages cost twice that. Nothing about this man proclaimed that he had money, but he obviously had plenty. She liked the fact that he didn't show it.

"What are you hoping to get out of your stay here?" she asked.

He shrugged. "I like northern California in the springtime. Where I come from, there aren't many trees. It'll be fun to look at the redwoods around here. Besides, I want to see what a fat farm is all about."

Shea frowned. She was too proud of the regimen at Estate Mendocino to let that remark pass. "*Fat farm?* This is a health and fitness resort."

"Fat farm," he corrected primly. "You ought to turn this place into something useful. Like an amusement park. Or a used-car lot. Or . . ."

"Now look," she began. "*Sir—*"

"Duke," he interjected.

"*Duke*, you have to have a positive attitude. . . ." She stopped talking, and her face contorted with pain.

He stood, swinging one long leg over the back of the chair in a graceful motion. "What's the matter? Something in the mud bite you?"

"Leg c-cramp," she managed between clenched teeth. "I ran t-ten miles tonight. Which is th-three miles more than usual."

"Women shouldn't run," he said. "Makes them too hard to catch. Stick it up here." With those unceremonious words he pointed to the edge of the tub.

"No. Really, I'll be—"

"Hoist that leg up or I'll go mud diving for it."

Shea hurt too badly to argue. With a sucking sound her left foot and leg popped out of the mud. She rested her foot on the tub's rim, and his large, blunt looking hands surrounded her mud-slicked ankle.

"Ugh," he offered with comical disdain. "If this ankle weren't so terrific, I'd toss it back into the mud pit and hope for a cleaner one next time."

"The calf. Rub the c-calf," she said in a pained whisper. *I'm ordering a man I just met to give me a massage.* Other thoughts of decorum fled as a second cramp grabbed at her muscles.

"I've always been good with animals. Com 'ere, calf." His hands slid up to her knee, then stroked downward in a slow and incredibly soothing motion. He enveloped the width of her foot in one large palm and gently pushed the foot upwards. His other hand went to the back of her knee, cupped the muscles, and stroked downward again.

Duke's eyes narrowed in concern at the feel of her smooth, supple leg. If the rest of her had this kind of touch appeal, she challenged a man's control. He liked challenges, but he'd never felt this kind of overwhelming greed for a stranger. He knew that he was coming on to her too quickly, but he couldn't help himself. "Better?" he asked in a troubled, soft voice.

"Better." Her face relaxed as the pain subsided. He continued to rub the back of her leg, and their eyes met. Shea's throat closed as an elemental sense of attraction passed in that long, quiet gaze. She pulled her leg away and submerged it in the mud again.

"I was just getting started," he protested mildly.

"I don't accept massages on the first date," she answered.

Duke heard the nervousness she tried so hard to hide. "I'm sorry," he murmured sincerely. "I'm not trying to make a move on you in the mud bath." It wasn't exactly true, but he didn't want to upset her. She smiled, but her wide, violet eyes assessed him shrewdly.

"You do this kind of thing often?" she asked bluntly.

"Rub women in mud baths? Nope."

"You know what I mean. Move fast and hope for results."

"No," he said with soft rebuke. Duke settled back in

the chair, took the towel from the back of it, and cleaned his hands as he watched her. He realized suddenly that the towel now smelled of roses and cream. "I'm a very old-fashioned man."

He said that without teasing, and she felt a little guilty. "I hear a lot of come-ons in my line of work," Shea explained. "Some of our male guests think sex is part of our program."

The look she got for that remark told her a lot about the man sitting across from her. He frowned in a contemplative, gentle way that indicated that she'd hurt him by categorizing him with other men. "*Querida*, don't judge a horse when he starts from the gate. Wait for him to go the distance."

She gave him a startled gaze while a sense of awe grew inside her chest. There was something about this stranger that was very easy to adore, something so powerful and instinctive that it frightened her. In twenty-nine years nothing like this had happened to her before.

"I apologize," she said crisply. "Would you please just leave?"

He nodded, stood up, and looked at her in a way that was both wistful and teasing. "I'll have to talk to the owner about these rules that say guests and staff can't fraternize." He shook his head in mild dismay. "Fraternize. That doesn't sound like much fun, anyway, eh, *querida*?"

"No," she agreed. Was he giving up? Shea wondered. Had she made it too clear that she wasn't going to break any rules? Why was he giving up so easily? When did life become so confusing? Life at Estate Mendocino was serene and beautiful. She liked life that way.

He bowed to her in a manner that was both funny and gallant. "Good night, Shea Somerton. I'll look forward to seeing you tomorrow, when you're mudless."

"Good night," she answered softly, laughing. He turned and walked toward the door. "You're taking the towel."

He had the pink hand towel, dabbed with mud, slung over his shoulder. He didn't seem to care that mud was getting on his white pullover. "I know," he told her.

"But . . ."

"I'm stealing it."

"Why?"

Duke turned at the doorway, gave her an enigmatic look, and simply smiled. The towel carried her scent, and he wasn't going to give it up.

"*Querida*, I'm just that kind of man. I take what I want."

He winked and left the room. Shea listened intently, her heart hammering in her throat, as his bootsteps padded down the carpeted hallway to the main door. After she heard the door open and close, she continued to sit still, feeling a little stunned. How long was he planning to stay at the resort? And what else would he charm away from her during that time, besides a hand towel?

The sun had just crested the rounded, tree-tufted mountains in the east as Shea walked down the flag-stone path from her cottage. One of the advantages of working at the resort was being able to live there amidst cultivated beauty that rivaled any setting in the world. Shea bent to brush an oak leaf off one of the lush azaleas that bordered the path. Though a team of gardeners cared for the estate, she was a perfectionist. Her attitude was a positive one, born out of a deep love for order.

When she reached the main building, she climbed marble steps to a long, deep veranda and entered the executive suite through double doors of gleaming glass and mahogany. Shea went to a small coat closet and traded her walking shoes for white leather flats.

"Good morning," Jennie Cadishio said from behind a stack of paperwork at her desk. "I've run out of computer paper. Everyone in the kitchen is having hysterics because the avocados are one day past the pinnacle of ripeness and the low-cal pâté isn't low-cal enough. Joanne Thurston wants someone to walk her poodle *four* times today. Anne says she can't reach the two o'clock aerobics class because she has a shin splint. And *I* have a lousy raccoon in my attic at home."

Shea went into her office and began raising the white wooden blinds that covered the tall windows. "Send someone from maintenance to town for the paper. Tell the kitchen to find some way to use the avocados and to forget about the pâté until they get it right. Have one of the gardeners walk Thurston's poodle. You'd think the woman had won the Oscar, the way she's acting. I'll teach the two o'clock class. As for your raccoon, I told you not to buy that ancient house in Mendocino. It's probably the ghost of a raccoon."

"You must have meditated an extra ten minutes this morning," Jennie called. "You're extraordinarily calm."

Shea made a tour of her large, white-and-tan office, plumping the hand-woven cushions on the visitors' chairs, brushing a speck of dust off the white bookcases. "I just want to be focused and relaxed for the meeting."

She shut the office door, smoothed a wrinkle in her turquoise jumpsuit, made sure that the clasp on her pearl necklace hadn't slipped around to the front and that the silver-and-pearl belt wasn't crooked, then sat down at her desk. To sidetrack her nervousness she picked up a guest list and began checking yesterday's staff notes.

Shea smiled. Chip Greeson, the game-show host, had been intercepted in the kitchen after lunch yesterday. He said he only wanted to take a peek at the facilities, but the staff suspected that he'd swiped a broiled pheasant for a snack. Angela Michaels, president of a Fortune 500 company called Angel Face Cosmetics, had offered one of the male fitness instructors much more than a makeover. He had tactfully declined.

Shea felt a twinge of guilt. After her encounter with the outrageous rascal last night, she could empathize with the instructor. Her face flushed as she recalled her traitorous inclination to be reckless. After the meeting her first order of business was to find out Duke's last name. The intercom buzzed on her phone.

"Mr. Araiza is here," Jennie told her.

Shea took a deep breath. Alejandro Araiza, the estate's new owner. "Thank you," she answered. "I'll be right out."

Shea leaped to her feet and went to the door, pulled it open, and stepped into the reception area wearing a welcoming smile. Alejandro Araiza held out one large, blunt hand as she came to a shocked stop.

"Call me Duke," he said warmly, and smiled.

Two

Shea was dimly aware of extending her hand, more aware that he grasped it in the same sensual, slow way he'd grasped her leg last night. He wore sleek black loafers, khaki trousers, a light-blue golf shirt, and a beige sport jacket with a fine black line in the weave. Gone was the darkly exotic *hombre*; in his place was a darkly exotic businessman. But his eyes were exactly the same as they appraised her—intense, gentle, *very* interested.

"Duke?" she repeated numbly.

He nodded. "Alejandro by birth certificate. Duke by nickname." His forefinger stroked the tender center of her palm, reassuring her. "Sorry. I like to play games. And last night I figured that you'd stiffen up even more if I told you who I was." His smile was utterly teasing and yet not the least bit arrogant. "I wouldn't have wanted anything else to cramp."

Shea glanced at Jennie, a redhead whose big eyes looked even bigger at the moment. Shea realized that Jennie was studying the handshake that had lingered far too long. Shea realized that she was squeezing

Alejandro "Duke" Araiza's hand much too intimately. She removed her hand and stepped back.

"Mr. Araiza," she said blankly, still absorbing his announcement.

"Duke," he corrected cheerfully.

"Of Solo Verde Farms. The man who owns Thoroughbred race horses."

He nodded. "I think that's me."

"The man who owns Spanish Outlaw."

"Winner of last year's Triple Crown. Yep." He tilted his head toward her office. "Let's go sit a spell and talk."

Sit a spell. Shea had the feeling that despite the change in clothes, Duke Araiza was as much homespun rancher as sophisticated businessman. Homespun, an *hombre*. That black hair, dark as the underside of night, shagged forward, an unruly and entirely intriguing contrast to his otherwise neat appearance.

"Yes," she managed to say as she led him into her office. Shea nearly jumped when he swung the door closed with a jaunty shove of one hand. "Please, sit down," she muttered. "Can I get you something?" She paused just long enough to smile grimly as she analyzed what he might say in return—knowing him—and hurried on. "Mineral water, herbal tea, fruit juice . . ."

"How about a cup of strong coffee with extra cream and sugar?"

Shea covered her chagrin with a neutral expression, then punched the intercom button. "Jennie, please have the kitchen send Mr. Araiza a cup of strong coffee with cream and extra honey."

"Uh, *sure*." Shea could hear the surprise in Jennie's voice. Coffee was verboten for the estate's guests and therefore in short supply.

"I'm sorry," Shea told him. "We don't keep sugar on the premises. Honey's the best we can do."

He had settled into a chair across from her gilded French desk, and now he crossed his legs and shrugged happily. "Sugar's not important right now." The way he looked at her made Shea feel that they both knew exactly what was important right now, and it had to do with the energy between them.

"This is incredible," she said softly as she sat down at her desk.

"What? That you don't keep sugar around? You can fix that. Don't worry."

Duke watched her clasp her hands on top of the ridiculously ornate desk and knew that she was still in shock. Even in shock, she looked fantastic. She had swept her blond hair up in one of those curly styles that defied gravity, and the color of the jumpsuit accented her eyes. With her pearl necklace and small pearl earrings she radiated elegance. Duke remembered the witty, spontaneous way she'd dealt with him last night and wondered if the elegance was a front for a delightfully earthy nature. He intended to find out.

"I don't mean to look dumbfounded," she said carefully. "It's just that I had no idea what to expect about the new owner. I wasn't told much. Sir Nigel has owned the estate for the past fifteen years and in the eight years I've been here, he hasn't stayed in close contact other than visiting a couple of times a year." She struggled for tactful words. "You've acquired the resort for . . . investment purposes?"

"Nope. I won it in a poker game."

Shea sat back slowly, drawing her hands into her lap, feeling the blood drain from her face. "A poker game?"

He smiled at her stunned reaction. "Nigel and I are horse-racing cronies. He bought a few colts from me, he comes to visit my ranch occasionally, and we play poker. A month ago, in a . . . well . . . a sort of hell raising mood, he tossed this place into the pot. And I had a straight flush."

Shea had enough poker savvy to know why Duke Araiza looked so proud of that hand. "So you . . . you just *won* the resort? You didn't even want it?"

He shrugged again, his eyes roaming over her in a distracted way. "I want it more, now that I'm here." He gave her just enough time to ponder the insinuation in that remark, then went on. "Tell me about yourself. You've been here eight years?"

"Since I graduated from college. Well, actually, before that. I came up here during college to work summers as an instructor. The former manager offered me a full-time job after I got my degrees."

"Degrees?" he repeated curiously.

"One in nutrition. One in physical education."

"P.E. You're a jock!"

She couldn't help smiling. "I guess so." The smile faded. "Could you tell me what plans you have for the estate?"

"Don't know." He raised both hands in a nonchalant gesture, then let them fall into his lap. "I just wanted to see what a fat farm was all about, first."

Shea felt the anxiety beginning to build. "It's a health and fitness resort, Mr. Araiza. . . ."

"Duke."

"Duke. Uhmmm, what would you like to know? We show a profit every year—not a large one, but then, Sir Nigel never looked on the estate as a money-making—"

"Ah, I don't care about that stuff. I want to know more about you. When did you become head honcho?"

"Four years ago, when the former manager retired."

"And you live in that little place over at the edge of the oak grove, that place with all the rose bushes?"

"Yes. That's the manager's cottage."

"Suits you. Roses suit you. Now"—he rubbed his hands together enthusiastically—"about that rule that says staff and guests can't fraternize? I don't think that applies to you and me. As the owner, I hereby decree that it doesn't. How about going to dinner with me tonight?"

Shea took a deep breath and tried to control her anger. She rose and walked to a window, then stood staring out at the estate's golf course, an emerald carpet that stretched into the distance. "Does my job depend on the answer?" she asked grimly.

Suddenly, it felt as if the room's air had cooled to arctic levels. "No," came his slow, husky reply. "*Querida*, you're a little too defensive."

She turned quickly, her hands clasped rigidly behind her back. "I apologize. But I don't know what to make of all this. I want to cooperate with the new owner, but I don't think the new owner gives a damn about this place." Shea took a deep breath. "I don't think you like it, or understand it, or want to preserve it."

He rose to his feet, a towering, masculine presence in her rose-scented, delicate office. Shea wasn't accustomed to feeling short—not at five-seven—but now she felt tiny.

"You're right. I don't understand this place," he confirmed in an annoyed voice. "I'm no Scrooge—God knows I enjoy spending money—but I've never seen anything like this playground for the Perrier-and-Rolls-Royce crowd. I'm not sure I like it, and I haven't decided yet whether it's worth preserving. Give me a little time."

Shea exhaled slowly. She held out both hands and realized abruptly that they were trembling. Duke Araiza had too much power over her.

"We indulge in some frivolous things here, I know," she admitted. "I won't try to defend classes like Zen for

Hiking. I won't defend the silly luxuries like our individually wrapped tooth brushes with the tooth paste already applied. Those things aren't important. What's important is that people leave here feeling happier and healthier than when they came. This place has a very special aura."

"For folks who can afford it," he said in a somber tone. Without warning, he crossed the short space between them and grasped her hands. "Relax," he told her. "Show me around and I'll try to act pampered." His expression softened, and a coy smile crooked one corner of a mouth that was strong and generous. "And cancel my coffee order. You make my adrenaline run too high as it is."

Shea laughed, realizing that he was much more open-minded than she'd thought. "It's mutual. You've rattled me."

As she watched with hypnotized fascination, he drew her hands to his mouth and kissed the back of each one, his dark gaze never leaving hers. His mouth was warm and pliant on her skin.

"Because you love this fancy gold mine and you think I'm about as out of place here as a mustang at a steeplechase," he prodded.

Shea nodded blankly. The man demanded truthfulness. "But maybe we need a little excitement around here."

"Maybe *you* need a little excitement."

"I like peace and quiet."

"I'm peaceful. I'm quiet."

"You're impossibly aggressive."

"I know a good thing when I see it." He let go of her hands and stepped back. "So take me on a tour, good thing."

Shea felt as if she were a horse that Duke Araiza was slyly attempting to gentle. She smiled thinly. He didn't know that under her tame facade she was as much a mustang as he was.

"This is one of the pools."

"Shea, how many pools do I own?"

"One Olympic-sized outdoor pool and two indoor pools, including this one."

"Don't forget the pool in my room."

"There are small pools in all the cottages."

"It's not big enough to swim in and not small enough to be a bathtub. What do people do in them?"

"Float," she answered lightly. "One of our guests, Prince Shalukan, brings an armada of toy battleships whenever he comes here, so that he can stage mock battles."

"Sounds like a tough guy. What country is he prince of?"

"Teresan. It's a little oil-rich island about the size of Vermont, located somewhere in the South China Sea. No threat to foreign military powers, that's for sure."

"What a relief," Duke noted drolly.

Shea watched as he put both brawny hands on his hips and gazed at the glistening indoor pool. A huge skylight filtered streaks of sunshine down onto the speckled blue tiles surrounding it. The pool was the central feature of a two-story atrium at the heart of the main building. A gallery of guest rooms circled it, fronted by a white balustrade. Ferns and flowering plants hung from brass arms on the gallery posts. Giant ficus trees in white, Romanesque pots sat around the pool.

"Smells like a jungle around here," he offered. "But I guess that's just because I'm not used to so many plants."

A dark-haired woman wearing a tiny pink bikini was asleep in a lounge chair by the water's edge.

"Who's the babe?" he asked. "Anybody I should ask for an autograph?"

Shea's mouth quirked in involuntary humor. Duke Araiza was the kind of man who couldn't care less about someone's status. He would ask for an autograph simply to flirt. "A Russian ballet star who defected. Now she directs one of the big New York dance companies."

"Oh, well, brunets aren't my style, anyway." He gave her a sincere, if rakish, appraisal. "I like muddy blondes."

"Indeed." Her mouth set in an unyielding line, warm reactions churning inside her, she led the way outdoors. "To your left," she told him, pointing to a sleek, stone building in the distance, "are the estate's stables. We have a fully staffed riding facility, and some guests have their own mounts flown in during their stays."

"Good Lord," he muttered. "I love my horses, but I don't take them on vacation with me."

"Would you like to see the Japanese garden next?"

"Sure. And then I'd like to see the replica of the Eiffel Tower, the Alamo, and—"

"Enough," she warned in mild reproach. He laughed deeply and shortened his long, powerful stride to match hers.

They walked down a neat walkway bordered by willow trees and carefully manicured shrubs. Shea spent the next few minutes describing the estate in detail.

"How many acres?" he asked finally.

"About five hundred."

"What a ranch this would make!"

Shea chewed her lower lip and said nothing. Her beautiful resort, a ranch? "Everything in the world doesn't have to be practical to be worthwhile," she muttered.

"I agree. I race horses for a living, remember? But there's something about this place. It says to the rest of the world, 'You can't come here. You're not important enough.' I grew up with that attitude being shoved down my throat because I was poor. I won't put up with it."

Shea shook her head. "We don't care about a guest's social status. Anyone who can pay the fees is welcome here."

"Oh? How many waitresses and mechanics have you got registered?"

He arched one black brow at her, and she sighed. "You're a hard man to influence."

Duke smiled. "Maybe you're not using the right tactics."

A few minutes later they stopped on a low ridge, far from the main estate grounds. Duke inhaled softly as he scanned a view straight from a Japanese silk painting. A small, delicately recreated Japanese pavilion stood at the center of the garden, surrounded by a serene arrangement of exotic trees and plants. Man-made waterfalls bubbled into shimmering pools, and even from here he could see the red *koi* fish swimming lazily in their depths. It was a place of such privacy and serenity that he immediately resolved to protect it. No matter what he decided about this ridiculous playground, the Japanese garden would never be harmed.

"Now, this," Shea whispered, "is my favorite place."

He turned to look at her with new admiration. Duke noticed the glistening reverence in her eyes. Her skin was the color of the pale, smooth flowers on the plants beside the pavilion. Her contentment was almost tangible, and it drew him in a way that went beyond physical attraction. He wanted to absorb her, to learn her inside and out.

She turned her face toward him, smiled, and looked

down at his feet. "You're tapping a toe again," she noted, remembering how he'd done that the night before. "What are you thinking about now?"

"That you belong here in a kimono, with a book of haiku open on your lap." *That you belong with me*, he added silently.

Her eyes filled with pleasure and surprise. "You like the garden?"

"Love it," he told her sincerely.

Pleasure infused her expression, and her smile nearly broke the limits of his control. It would be so easy to simply take her in his arms and kiss her.

She seemed to sense that and looked away, her eyes turned toward the ground again. "Watch your footing," she said softly, and pointed to the rough-hewn steps that led down the ridge to the garden. She moved gracefully ahead of him, her back very straight.

"I'm willing to take my time," he answered just as softly, and saw her head move in an unmistakable sign that his meaning had registered.

They walked silently through the garden listening to the sounds of the waterfalls and the throaty murmurs of birds in the surrounding forest. "Redwoods," Shea noted, waving a hand at the trees. "Small ones, by this area's standards. A lot of the redwoods have been logged at one time or other. This stand was cut down about thirty years ago, I've been told."

She sat down on a curved stone bench. Duke sat beside her, his knee casually brushing hers. He was aware that she didn't move away from the contact. But she faced forward, her hands clasped in her lap. This one was a hand clasper, that was for sure, he noted. First in her office as she sat at that fancy desk, and now. When he made her uncomfortable, she clasped. A point worth remembering.

"What's Mendocino like?" he asked calmly. "I bypassed it on the drive up."

"A transplanted New England town. Maine saltbox-style houses, Cape Cod cottages, most of it perched along a main street that fronts the Pacific. It began in the last century as a logging and shipping town, but now it's an artists' colony. Lots of inns, restaurants, galleries. A nice place. It's about ten miles from here." She looked at him curiously. "You drove here?"

"Yep. Like to drive. How do most folks get here?"

"We have a small plane that shuttles them up from San Francisco, or we send a limo to pick them up. Cisco's the nearest big city."

"I own an air field?" he asked incredulously.

"A little one." She pointed toward the western hills covered with a mixed forest of redwoods and oaks. "Beyond those." She started to stand. "If you want to see it, let's go get a golf cart."

"Later, later," he said, reaching out to grasp her wrist gently. She gave him a wary look and sat back down. Her skin felt like fine silk beneath his calloused fingers. Mud baths. Maybe they were worthwhile, he thought. Duke turned her hand palm up and studied it. "I see private colleges, debutante balls, and lots of marriage-minded young yuppies in your past."

"You're checking the wrong lines. I worked my way through UCLA with the help of a scholarship, I was never a deb, and yuppies, marriage-minded or otherwise, aren't my type. I'm a loner, I fear. Not very social."

"No man, ever?" He shook his head. "A beautiful, mature woman. No, it can't be."

"Which line tells you that?" Shea asked dryly.

"Male intuition."

"There was someone, a couple of years ago." Without thinking, gazing off into the distance, Shea turned her palm over and lightly grasped Duke Araiza's hand. "He wasn't a yuppie; he was a bohemian ex-hippie. He did woodworking; he made sculptures as well as utilitarian pieces such as bowls and furniture. He had a shop in Mendocino."

"You loved him?" Duke asked, carefully hiding his surprise.

"We were . . . very close. He was the most gentle, the sweetest man. . . ."

"But you didn't love him." Duke knew he was on the verge of sounding both rude and nosy, but he had a gut wrenching need to learn whether she'd ever been in love before.

"I loved him enough to grieve for months after he was killed," she answered softly.

"Killed?" Duke gently rubbed the back of her hand with this thumb.

She nodded. "He liked to roam the woods." A bitter cast came over her features. "He was accidentally shot by a hunter. It was one of those awful accidents that happens almost every year during deer season."

"Shea, I'm sorry I pried. . . ."

"It's all right." She looked at him calmly, her violet eyes almost grateful. "Everyone who knew him wants to forget that he ever existed, and I never get to talk about him anymore. If feels *right* to discuss him with you. You look like a good listener."

"That's because I want to know everything about you."

She was disconcerted by that remark and squinted at him in mild rebuke.

"Want to change the subject?" he asked.

"Yep." She mimicked his way of talking, which bordered on a John Wayne drawl.

"Folks still living?"

"Nope."

"Want to talk about mumsy and daddy?"

"Nope."

Duke sighed. "The lady becomes a clam on personal subjects." But at least she was holding his hand as if she'd never let go. "Okay, what's it like to be manager of this prissy sand trap? What do you have to do?"

"Supervise reservations, supervise a staff of about fifty people, supervise one hundred and twenty-three guests." She gave him a challenging look. "We're always booked months in advance. We don't even have to advertise to do it. We have that kind of prestigious reputation."

"Well, la di da," he said dryly, crooking one brow at her superior tone. "What do the well-off and well padded do once they get here?"

"They're not here to lose a lot of weight. We don't even talk about that. We emphasize healthy eating and good fitness routines. The guests hike, they do aerobics, they practice stress reduction techniques, they have massages. In short, they learn better habits and relax."

"Sounds like a lot of work just to relax."

"So, hulk, what's your health and fitness regimen?" She pulled her hand away. He took it back.

"Ranch work. Burritos. Good beer. Try it. It'll keep your mind straight and your stomach flat."

"I have a straight mind and a flat stomach, and I wouldn't encourage anyone to follow your suggestions."

He heard the laughter low in her voice and knew that she was less stern than her words. "What kind of gal are you hiding under there?" he teased, peering into her eyes. Their violet depths were much warmer and more inviting than she suspected.

"One who is very happy with her life the way it is."

"You still alone?"

"Not at the moment. I'm in the company of a very inquisitive man."

"You lonely?"

"Ah." Shea looked up at the sky overhead, watching white clouds floating against the blue background. "Are you?"

"Ah. She changes the attack to suit herself." Duke was silent for a moment. Then he said thoughtfully, "Yep." When she gazed at him with surprise, he continued, "There have been people to keep me company, but not people to keep me from feeling alone."

Her expression took on a sympathetic cast.

Mesmerized, Duke told her, "I'm used to being alone, but I don't have to like it. I was married once, a long time ago, but I was alone even then. I'm thirty-six years old, and I don't want to spend the rest of my life putting up Christmas trees by myself."

"Christmas trees?" she asked softly.

He nodded. "That's when you really know that you're missing something. When you put up a Christmas tree and there's nobody important to help you do it."

Shea swallowed tightly. He had touched a deeper chord than he'd ever know. She thought of all the holidays she'd spent in the dingy little apartment she and her mother had shared in a run-down area of Los Angeles.

"When I was a child," she told him softly, "I put up a lot of Christmas trees by myself. My mother was always at work, and when she wasn't, well, she didn't take much interest."

"What about your father?"

"I was about five years old when he left home for good."

Duke frowned, studying her, trying to unravel the elegant exterior and learn more about her intriguing past. He started to ask her if she had any brothers or sisters, but she shook her head and held up one hand.

"Enough. Suffice it to say, I dislike holidays. Let's change the subject."

Duke squeezed her hand. "You look so sad. I didn't mean to do that to you."

"Oh, you didn't," she answered quickly, trying to hide her unhappiness. "You're *too* good as a listener. I keep forgetting that we just met. I'm talking too much."

"You look like a person who doesn't talk enough. It's all right to open up to me. I never kiss and tell."

She smiled crookedly and gave him a grateful look. To his surprise her eyes filled with tears. "*Hombre*, you're stealing my good sense," she murmured. "So you never kiss and tell?" She leaned forward, closed her eyes, and brushed her mouth lightly over his.

Duke warned himself not to take advantage of the situation, but her kiss was such a tempting mixture of gentleness and restrained passion that it overwhelmed his judgment. As he felt her easing away, he slipped an arm around her waist. He watched her eyes open, wide with shock. "Easy, now. Easy," he whispered soothingly. Then his mouth was on hers, warm and tight.

He heard her murmur of protest, but she didn't move away. If she meant to rebuff him, she failed, because her mouth was pliant. If she meant to show no desire, it was a lost cause, because she sighed eagerly against his lips. He had never tasted anything as sweet, and the scent of roses and cream mingled with the kiss to envelope him in sensation. Deep inside he shivered and couldn't stop—didn't want to stop—the male reaction that brought every nerve ending to arousal.

Shea was collapsing inside, part of her protesting that this wasn't proper because she worked for the man and had to keep a professional distance, part of her protesting that it had been too long since she'd been kissed, that she'd never been kissed like this.

Who could run from the promise of his perfectly seductive mouth?

He slid his tongue between her lips and explored her delicately, expertly. Shea knew only that she was kissing him back and that her hand was rhythmically squeezing his. When he drew his hand away and clasped her side just beneath one breast, she pulled back, groggy with confusion and burning all over. "Thank you," she managed to say huskily. "But I think that will be enough."

His face was so close that she could see the gold flecks in his dark eyes. The gold was nearly the color of her hair, and she wondered if it was a sign that perhaps this instant connection between the two of them was meant to be. Shea tried to ignore such whimsy. He was her employer. He was here to wreak havoc, and suddenly it occurred to her that he needed her cooperation.

"You're always so proper and polite," he whispered. "It makes me want to tempt you even more."

"Will it be easier this way?" she asked in a low, wounded voice. "If you seduce me, will it be easier for you to do what you want with the estate?"

Dismay filtered into his gaze, dulling the gold, turning his eyes into black warnings. "You should have stopped with 'Thank you, but that will be enough,' " he said in a low, rebuking voice. "It would have been perfect."

He let go of her and sat back, looking tired and disappointed. After several awkward seconds in which they eyed each other remorsefully, he said, "I can tell, *querida*, that you and I have a lot of trust to build."

Shea's head drooped. She felt drained. "Life doesn't move very fast here. I don't move very fast either. I apologize for provoking what happened. I apologize for being so suspicious."

"Sssh. As you said last night, I'm one fast *hombre*."

The self-effacing tone of his voice made her look up at him with a tentative smile. He smiled back, though his gaze still held a rebuke. "But I'm not manipulative. If you tell me never to touch you again, I'll honor that. And your job will be very safe."

Shea couldn't bring herself to tell him that. "Can't we just slow down?" she asked wearily. "Do you have to make everything so complicated so quickly?"

He laughed, and the pleasure in his eyes showed how much her answer meant to him. "I'll be a good guest, how about that? And keep an open mind. We'll be friends."

"Friends," she agreed immediately. She *had* to convince this man to leave well enough alone, at least as far as the estate was concerned.

"Friends," Duke repeated. He would challenge her to keep up with him and tempt her to run wild.

Three

"Down and two and down and three and flow with the music and down and four and stretch, stretch." Shea made her voice drop to a throaty and relaxed timbre as the gentle Chopin etude began to slow. "Now reach toward the ceiling, reach, reach, and let all that negative energy and anxiety flow out of you. You're relaxed, you're happy, you've just been good to yourself. Now *exhale*."

What sounded behind her in the aerobics room weren't so much exhalations of soothed psyches but groans of relief. Shea turned and bowed to the two-dozen exercisers, male and female, who were already staggering toward a water cooler in the corner.

"The Marines could use you!" someone called, and appreciative laughter confirmed that others felt the same way.

Shea smiled apologetically. She tried to balance the intensity of her nature with a serene attitude, but where exercise was concerned, intensity always won out. "Your regular teacher will be back tomorrow."

"There *is* a God!"

Shea took a towel from atop the stereo deck next to her and dabbed at her face as she joined the group at the cooler. Glenda Farrar, all pink and a little pudgy in a purple, one-piece leotard, sidled up to her and whispered, "I want to be in the four-o'clock class tomorrow."

Shea looked down at the tiny, fiftyish brunet and saw girlish excitement in her eyes. Mrs. Farrar, a widow who operated a children's boutique in Beverly Hills, was a lonely, shy, adorable little cream puff who had something up her sleeve besides a sweaty arm.

"Certainly, Mrs. Farrar."

"And do you, could you . . ." Mrs. Farrar looked around furtively to make certain that no one was listening. "Could you arrange for me to sit at Mr. Steinberg's table for dinner this evening?"

Ah-hah. So Mrs. Farrar had designs on Dan Steinberg, a retired business executive and decidedly distinguished looking widower. Dan Steinberg was in the four o'clock aerobics class, Shea recalled. "I'll pull some strings and make certain of it," Shea whispered.

The pink face lit up. "Thank you!"

"Shea?"

Shea turned to see Mark Langman, the estate's coordinator of guest services, shifting uncomfortably at the doorway of the aerobics room. She walked over quickly, a little worried by his attitude. "What's wrong?"

Mark, a blond giant with a physique to rival Sylvester Stallone's, spoke in a distressed whisper. "Chip Greeson was plastered in the massage room a little while ago."

"Plastered?"

"Soused. Happy. Lit like a light bulb. He tried to act cool, but the staff smelled tequila on him. He was so loose he didn't *need* a massage."

Shea rubbed her forehead wearily. "Where is he now?"

"He rambled off to his room for a nap." Mark shifted

again, a hulk in distress. "Shea? After lunch someone saw him with Mr. Araiza. You might check with Mr. Araiza . . ."

"I see," Shea said crisply, her mouth tightening. That explained everything, probably. "I'll check with *Mr. Araiza* to find out if he noticed anything. Where is Mr. Araiza now?"

"Uh, as far as I know, he's asleep in a lounge chair by the outdoor pool. He took one of the horses for a ride all morning."

"He was scheduled for a yoga class and nutrition counseling."

"He canceled. About Mr. Greeson—"

"We're not here to play nursemaid," Shea said wearily. "Tell the staff to just forget about the incident in the massage room. It won't happen again." *Duke Araiza, that hombre!* Chip Greeson had been a model guest in the past.

Twenty minutes later, after showering and changing from her leotard and tights into a flowing white sundress, Shea marched out to the pool. It lay like a rectangle of blue light, surrounded by plush white furniture and potted orange trees. A canopied bar was set up at the far end, staffed with a bartender who served nothing stronger than papaya juice.

Duke was stretched out on a lounge chair, dark aviator glasses covering his eyes, his arms behind his head. Despite her anger, Shea slowed as she approached him. A warning fluttered in her chest, telling her that she couldn't ignore his physical appeal. She could barely resist his emotional appeal, either, the danger he promised as well as the tenderness. She had known danger in her early years, had avoided it in all the years since, and only now realized that a part of her craved it.

He wore blue swim trunks that accentuated the weathered, bronzed beauty of his skin and revealed all but a small portion of that skin to the world. Soft looking black hair was slicked to his lean, strong thighs, and a thick patch of it covered his chest. That chest and his arms were masterpieces of muscle. Shea swept one more awed gaze over his body and came to a stop beside his chair, her face flushed. She snatched a nearby chair and plunked it down. He yawned.

"Duke, you'd better be awake," she said firmly.

"Uhmmm?"

Suddenly he was awake. His head turned toward her and a slow, heart-stopping smile slid across his mouth. Dear Lord, why did the man have to have such a friendly smile?

"*Buenas tardes*," he murmured in a sleepy, seductive voice, "my *querida*."

"Good afternoon. Do you know why Chip Greeson is drunk?"

"Oh." He pulled the back of his lounger to the upright position.

"Oh? I smell a rat."

"I smell orange trees. And I smell your perfume. Damn, Shea, that kind of tantalizing perfume ought to sold with a warning label: May Attract Ranchers Who Have Noble but Wild Intentions. I dream about the way you smell. . . ."

"Duke," she said threateningly.

He rubbed his stomach languidly, and her eyes followed the movement of his broad hand on the flat, taut surface. Duke Araiza, who had probably never used a weight machine or taken an aerobics class, was six-plus feet of prime male muscle. He grinned at her and she tore her gaze away. He spoke contritely. "I sat at Chip's table during lunch—if you can call that bland little bit of fish and green stuff lunch—and we struck up a conversation. Did you know that he used to be a news anchorman in San Diego before he became a game-show host? I've always said that those newspeople were entertainment oriented."

"Do you have tequila on the premises?"

He yawned. "Well, Chip likes to have an occasional shot or two, and he misses that when he comes here . . . so, we went over to my place and watched a rerun of his show and had a couple of drinks. He looked so happy that I gave him the bottle and a candy bar. I'm not responsible for whatever he did after that."

Shea exhaled a long breath. "Duke, his wife sends him here to be *healthy* for a week."

"*Miserable*. He only comes here to please her."

Her mouth popped open in shock. "No! He's a model guest."

"Yep." Duke raised the back of his chair, sat up, and removed his glasses. His dark eyes shimmered with regret as he analyzed her shock. "*Querida*, the man's very happy the way he is. He sneaks food and booze into his room all the time. Go easy on him."

Shea crossed her arms and studied him sternly. "I'm not as upset at Mr. Greeson as I am at you. What other contraband do you have in your cottage?"

He squinted one eye at her. "If you want to check my place out, you're welcome to come over tonight and do it."

Shea inhaled sharply. "All right, I will. I thought you were going to try to fit into the routine here so that you'd see how beneficial it is."

"I am fitting in. But a little tequila and a few candy bars never hurt anybody, in moderation."

She stood up, her fists clenched. "I'll be over after dinner to collect your treasures. Until you decree otherwise, I'm going to run this estate the way it's always been run."

Duke let his chair down again and replaced his sunglasses. The set of his mouth told her that he was cheerful. "Me and my treasures will be waiting."

The cottages were miniature versions of the main house, tiny French chateaux tucked among towering oak trees, the ultimate in privacy and luxury. As dusk gathered around her, Shea limped up the cobblestone walkway. She had had a long day, and her evening run had only resulted in a pulled calf muscle. Damn Duke Araiza for complicating her life!

The cottage had a small garage, and its door stood open. Shea stopped and stared at the red Ferrari sitting inside.

Duke opened the cottage's front door quickly when she knocked. He wore jeans and a white gold shirt. His feet were bare. His eyes flickered with anticipation and delight, making her nervous. "Welcome to the lair of the hedonist," he said as he swept a hand toward the interior.

"I won't bother you for long."

"No bother."

The cottages had all been redecorated in the past year by experts brought in from Beverly Hills, and this particular cottage was the crowning glory. The ambiance was decidedly masculine but not rustic. Early American with class, the decorator had said. It suited Duke, Shea decided. A shallow blue pool occupied the back half, not far from a double bed on a raised redwood platform. The pool, as he had said earlier, wasn't large enough to swim in, but it was perfect for lazy floating.

The lights were low, and soft jazz played on a tape deck near the bed. He followed her as she strolled through the cottage, her hands clasped behind her back. "One of your horses?" she asked, pointing to a photograph laying amid paperwork on a small desk.

"Uh-huh. Lady Be Good."

"I'll try my best," she noted dryly. "Where's the contraband?"

"Why are you limping?"

Shea turned to look up at him. "I ran too far, trying to work out my aggressions."

"Aggressions against me?"

"Frankly, yes."

He shook his head and said huskily, "You push yourself too hard."

"I like being fit."

"I think you like staying occupied so that you won't feel empty inside. People who devote so much time to one thing, excluding everything else in their lives, are usually avoiding something."

"Thank you, Dr. Duke Freud, but I feel very fulfilled."

"Well, let's see what we can do about that leg. I like your sundress, by the way. I meant to tell you at the pool, but you were mad at me. And I like the way you fix your hair, even if I can't figure out what in hell holds it on top of your head that way."

"A thirty-nine-cent hair band and two little barrettes."

He raised both hands and formed an expression of mock dismay. "Don't ruin the mystery!"

"I don't like mystery."

"Ah, a practical woman in an impractical job."

"Health-and-fitness counseling is *very* practical."

"Relaxing and having a good time is practical. This place goes way beyond that. Don't stay mad at me. Sit down and cool off."

She didn't like the blunt way he had of changing subjects. "I'm still mad at you."

"I'm the boss. You should do what I say, and I say sit

on the couch so that I can rub your calf again. Nothing personal, I assure you."

Shea eyed him for a moment. "I'm still taking the tequila and candy bars when I leave," she warned.

"Fair enough. Now relax."

She went to a dark gray couch in one corner and settled warily on one end of it. He sat down and patted his knee. "Foot up."

"I feel like a filly with a bad hoof."

"A pretty filly. A pretty hoof."

She gingerly placed her ankle on his knee. Looking suspiciously like a man who was trying to appear unmoved, he slid her white sandal off and began rubbing her foot.

"My foot's not hurt. My calf muscle is hurt," she directed.

"I like to work my way up. Prop yourself on those pillows and mellow out."

Shea propped herself up on two large pillows with bright Navajo designs, and she sank into their luxurious depths. She watched Duke as he looked at her foot, his eyes tracing every movement his fingers made. *He* was mellow, damn him, and *she* was a bundle of nerves.

"How did you get the scar across your nose?" she asked finally.

"In a fight, when I was, oh, about seventeen."

"I thought perhaps a horse kicked you."

"A lot of them have." He laughed softly. "But a lot of my fellow *hombres* have taken a jab or two at me, also."

"You like to fight?"

"Used to. Used to fight and raise all kinds of hell. Grew out of it."

"I hadn't noticed."

He laughed again. "*Querida*, my father was Spanish.

I have hot Mediterranean blood. I can't help but cause trouble."

"How did your father end up in southern California?"

"He never made it to southern California. He was an art exporter based in Madrid. He and my mother met in Mexico. She was a secretary at the embassy in Mexico City."

"Sounds romantic."

He smiled a little thinly and shook his head. Watching his profile, Shea saw his face tighten. "They had a shotgun wedding. My grandpa came down and made certain that my mother had a husband *before* she had a baby."

"You?"

"Yep. And then grandpa brought my mother home."

"Your grandfather was Mexican-American?"

"Yep. He came to the United States as a boy, worked as a ranch hand, and eventually bought his own place. The Solo Verde. I inherited it."

"You were born there?"

His hands rose to her ankle, drawing lines along the bones. "Such delicacy," he murmured. "Yep. Born on the ranch and grew up on the ranch. My mother was killed in a car accident when I was four. My grandfather was too busy to play parent, so I grew up as I pleased. Wild."

Shea's leg felt heavy and deliciously warm. The sensation, she acknowledged with surprise, was drifting over the rest of her body. Did Duke have magic in those large calloused hands? "What reformed you?" she asked.

"When I was eighteen, a horse fell on me. While I was recuperating, I went to work at a Thoroughbred ranch near us. I was too busted up to do real work, but I had a way with horses, and they let me supervise a couple of colts. So that was the start of my career in horse racing. I bought a colt of my own, won a little money, bought some more stock . . ."

"And now you've got one of the best-known operations in the country."

He looked up and grinned. "Proud of it, if I do say so myself."

"I can understand why you're proud."

A look of gentle surprise lit his handsome features. "I know that you grew up a lot different from me."

"Not really. I can understand." Shea looked away quickly. She'd grown up under circumstances that were probably rougher than his own. "My mother didn't have a lot of money. I didn't have a silver-spoon childhood."

"What is Shea Somerton all about?" he asked suddenly, his voice soft and low. "Behind those big violet eyes is she happy being such a tame filly?"

Shea looked back at him. *Could he read minds?* "My blood pressure's terrific, my pulse is great, I can run a seven-minute mile and bench press more than my own weight. I sleep well, I have a lot of energy, and I look forward to going to work in the morning."

"None of which necessarily says that you're happy. What about your social life?"

"I have friends on the staff. I have hobbies." She smiled at him primly. "I play the flute."

"Sounds like a boring life to me."

Shea opened her mouth, shut it, and silently admitted that her life *was* boring. Boring, but serene. "I like it," she said.

"Your shoulders are all hunched up."

"That's because you make me cranky and tense. I'm going to get a massage after I leave here."

"I give *great massages*. Ask any injured horse on my ranch. Lay down on your stomach and let me rub your shoulders." When she started to protest, he held up a finger and said coyly, "You're not *afraid* of me, are you?"

She knew that she'd been offered a challenge, one that she couldn't refuse. She wasn't afraid of the man; she was afraid of what the man could do to her ordered life and emotions. That was different, wasn't it?

"Hmmmph," she mumbled, then turned to lay on her stomach and snuggle her face into the pillows. As she fiddled with her dress, tucking it tightly around her legs like a shield, Shea told herself that she was accommodating him for the estate's sake. She had to keep him happy.

But she quivered when he sat down on the edge of the couch, his hard, lean hip and thigh pressed closely against her side. His hands settled on her bare shoulders, brushing aside wisps of hair. He molded his fingers to her skin and began to rub gently, circling, his touch sure and firm and incredible. Shea sighed with involuntary delight.

"Like that, do you?" he asked in a devilish voice.

"I envy your horses."

He laughed seductively.

She was being hypnotized, Shea thought blankly. She couldn't move . . . didn't want to move.

"I've been talking to the staff," Duke said, his voice almost a whisper. "They're crazy about you. You do a great job here, they tell me."

"They're happy because I'm a soft touch. I stay off people's backs as long as things run smoothly."

"It's more than that. Someone told me about Anna Fitzsimmons."

"Uhmmm. I just helped her out of a tough spot. I would have helped anyone on the staff that way."

"You sent her to a drug rehab program at the estate's expense."

Shea had her head turned to one side. She raised it

and looked at him warily over her shoulder. "I did. Sir Nigel let me use the budget any way I wanted. When I told him about Anna, he wasn't upset by my decision. Are you?"

"No."

"Oh." Feeling embarrassed by the accusing tone she'd used, Shea frowned as she lowered her head back to the pillow.

"Sssh, *querida*. I'm not a monster. I admire the way you run this place. I admire your compassion for people." His thumbs drew lines of delectable fire down the center of her spine. "No matter what I think about this resort, I like you."

"I like you, too," she mumbled, giving in to a mixture of relaxation and desire that made it difficult to think straight. "Dammit."

"Now that's what I want to hear. Don't be polite to me. Let yourself go. Who knows what kind of wonderful wildness you're hiding?" He laughed so softly that the sound was barely more than a rumble in his chest. "So you didn't grow up rich and fancy. I'm glad. Means we have more in common."

He leaned forward and kissed the back of her neck. The breath caught in Shea's throat and she bit her lower lip to keep from crying out with pleasure. His mouth was damp and hot; he trapped her skin between his teeth and nibbled, then moved to a different spot and did the same to it.

"I could eat you up," he whispered, his breath tickling her. "I knew that the minute we met. And I think you'd like for me to try."

Shea realized abruptly that she was trembling and that her whole body felt flushed and limp. "What I'd like," she whispered back, "and what would be right, are two different things. You and I are at odds over the estate. And you're my employer."

He trailed slow kisses down her spine and spoke in between them. "What happens . . . to Estate Mendocino . . . has nothing to do . . . with what fate has planned for you and . . . me."

Shea rolled over onto her back, intending to say that he was wrong, that the estate was her pride and joy—no, more than that, it was her sanctuary, the embodiment of the daydreams that had seen her through so many rough years as a youngster. But she gazed up at him and forgot every word. She had seen passion in men's eyes before but never anything as compelling and tender as the look in his. Shea dimly heard herself make a small, encouraging sound.

He shivered visibly and slipped his arms under her. Cradling her, he never stopped looking into her eyes, and the look tore her reserve apart. Shea cupped her hands around his face and pulled him to her. This time need mingled with sweetness, and his mouth was open and intimate when she lifted hers to it. Their tongues touched and explored. His arms tightened around her, and her fingers sank deeply into his thick black hair.

"We're not going to make love," he whispered. "Not tonight, anyway."

Breathing hard, Shea murmured in a puzzled tone, "You are the most confusing man."

He dropped kisses across her face and down one side of her neck. "I just want you to stop wondering how far you can let yourself go. I just want you to relax and enjoy being touched by me. Lord, Shea, I love kissing you and touching you. That's harmless enough, isn't it, *querida*?"

"Harmless," she murmured as his mouth seared a trail of kisses across her throat. Oh, this sweet, stubborn man made her want to cry for all the pleasure she'd never known until this moment. Was all the joy in the world, all the joy she'd waited for, embodied in Duke Araiza? He made it so easy to be wild, and he understood her need for caution even better than she understood it herself.

He slipped his hands up her back and hooked his fingers into the bodice of her strapless sundress. For one long moment he searched her eyes, seeing the uncertainty there but also the desire. "Tell me to stop and I will," he assured her. "I swear. You're in control."

"Harmless," she murmured again. She was out of control and enjoying every minute of it. "A little more would be . . . harmless."

Smiling tenderly, he pulled her bodice down below her breasts. Shea watched, mesmerized by the exquisitely happy look that came over his face as he studied her nakedness.

"I believe in quality, not quantity," she noted in a droll tone.

Duke heard the tentative, vulnerable undercurrent she tried to hide. His gaze rose to hers. "*Querida*, your quality will never go unnoticed by me."

Then he ducked his head and began kissing her breasts fervently, growling as he did. His actions were so comical and yet so sensual that Shea laughed even as her body arched upward in response. This man was a connoisseur who made her feel precious.

"Sometime soon I'm going to kiss the rest of your body this way," he told her huskily. "You're going to want me the way I want you," he added just before his lips closed over one pink nipple.

"I want you," she said, "but there's so much to consider."

He continued to drive her delightfully frantic with his skillful attention. His hands stroked her hips and thighs over the sundress, then dipped under her to raise her torso to his mouth once more.

"I'll give you time, *querida*," he promised. "But never forget that sometimes a man and a woman look at each other and see the future. That's what we see."

He sat up and pulled her with him, holding her tight in his arms as he whispered her name and kissed her forehead. After a moment of indecision she pushed him away gently.

"No more," Shea begged. "The future frightens me. You're only going to be here a few days. . . ."

"And those things don't matter. What matters is that we've got a pull between us, a need to connect, like the sky and the ground during a thunderstorm."

"Any relationship we'd have would be about that calm."

"Who needs calm? Why should everything be calm?"

"I like calm."

"Then let's try it." He let go of her with a slowness that showed how reluctant he was. Duke carefully pulled her bodice back into place. "Lay back on the pillows. Close your eyes."

Shea did as he asked. The pillows were soft and textured under her head, and she could smell the pleasant musk of Duke's skin as his fingertips began to stroke her forehead. He touched her lightly, drawing his fingers back and forth, the contact like the caress of a tantalizing breeze.

"I think you have the prettiest face," he said eventually. "Whoops. Close those eyes. Don't stare at me like a rope-shy mare. There. That's right. Close 'em. Yeah, smile a little. I like your smile. I'm gonna call you Sophia."

"Why?" Shea murmured languidly.

"You're got a mouth like Sophia Loren. Smooth. Ripe."

"Sounds like a piece of fruit."

"Sssh. You don't know how to let a man enjoy you."

"I've been on my own a long time. Independent, self-sufficient, all that."

"Me too. You don't have to give up those things to fall in love, do you? Hey! Close those eyes! Close 'em! I did it again. I said too much."

Her eyes shut but her thoughts racing, Shea asked, "Love?"

"Love at first sight, as far as I'm concerned."

It was too much. She'd never felt loved in her entire life, and the idea that this remarkable man was sincere caused her to open her eyes wide. Duke cupped her chin in one hand, leaned forward, and kissed her mouth slowly, possessively, before he settled back and smiled at her. "I move fast, I know."

"That's putting it mildly." The worst thing was that, Shea admitted silently, she was thrilled by what he'd said. She'd known Duke Araiza two days, he was here to look over with the estate and perhaps change it, he was a total outlaw, and yet she felt giddy because deep down she wanted him more than she'd ever wanted anyone in her life. Everything was out of control, and her serenity was shot to hell.

"Love is a dangerous word, amigo," she said in a taut, sad voice. "And one that I'm not very comfortable with."

"You will be," he promised.

"Where are the tequila and the candy bars?" she demanded. "I have to go. I . . . where are they?"

Frowning at her turbulent emotions Duke got up and went to a cabinet in the cottage's minikitchen. He retrieved a brown paper bag and brought it to her. Shea got up and took it, giving him a formal little nod of thanks as she did.

"I suppose it would do me no good to ask which member of my staff you're bribing to bring you this stuff," she told him.

"That's right. It's wonderful being the owner. People let me have almost anything I want."

"I suppose you're going to get a new supply tomorrow?"

He gave her a challenging, teasing look. "Could be. Guess you'll have to come back tomorrow night and check for it."

Shea squinted at him and spoke a few short words in Spanish.

"You must have Latin blood in you," he countered. "Someday I want to find out where you learned to sass people like that."

"*Adios*," she muttered.

He opened the door and Shea walked out without looking back. She felt as if she'd been dipped in hot gold and was only now being allowed to cool.

"Oh, *querida*, by the way," he called, "I'll be here for more than a few days. I've decided to stay for two weeks." He'd just made that decision, but he wasn't going to tell her so. She was beginning to relax, and all he needed was time.

Four

"This dining room gives me heartburn," Chip Greeson said to Duke as he shuttled a spoonful of whole-grain cereal and soy milk from a china bowl to his mouth. "Doesn't it remind you of Marie Antoinette's damned boudoir or something?"

Duke eyed the portly, white-haired game-show host affectionately. "Can't say," Duke told him drolly. "Never made acquaintance with that lady's boudoir."

"Well, hell, me neither," Chip answered with a grunt. "But you know what I mean. Satin drapes on the walls, prissy little chairs with bowed legs, lots of flowers. Always feels damned funny to sit here in my jogging suit."

Duke glanced down at his own outfit, well-worn gray sweatpants and a blue T-shirt with Santa Anita—Race Track of Champions printed on the chest. He grinned at Chip. "Pal, at least *your* suit matches," he noted. "And it's purple, which seems to be the 'in' color around here."

"*Mauve*, friend, not *purple*. You've got to use Beverly Hills lingo in this joint. *Mauve*. Yeah, all the designers are pushing mauve this spring, my wife says. She bought this for me. Told me not to come home until it's baggy." He laughed. "Good thing she was kidding."

"Good morning. May Dan and I join you?"

Glenda Farrar, wearing a mauve jogging suit with rhinestone butterflies appliquéd on the padded shoulders, beamed down at Duke. He stood up politely and Chip followed. "Why, certainly," Duke said. He glanced at Chip, and they shared a secret look of amusement. *More mauve.* Dan Steinberg was a tall, sternly handsome man with gray wings in his hair. Duke noted that his jogging suit was white. *Maybe Steinberg's a renegade,* he decided wryly.

After Steinberg introduced himself, he grasped Duke's outstretched hand. They shook, and Duke noted that the man had a limp, soft grip. *Bad sign,* Duke thought. *Hope he's worth Glenda's efforts.*

Everyone sat down, and a waiter hurried over to take the newcomers' breakfast orders. As he left, Duke caught Glenda Farrar looking at him. *It's working,* the matronly brunet mouthed quickly, nudging her eyebrows in Steinberg's direction. *Thank you.*

Duke bit back a smile and winked at her. *Sweet little doll,* he thought for perhaps the hundreth time. He and she had struck up a conversation by the pool yesterday, and he'd given her some advice on how to catch Steinberg's attention. She'd looked aghast at some of his suggestions, but she'd obviously geared up her courage and used them. Duke had promised to give her some more pointers today.

"Quit stalling and eat your cereal, Mr. Araiza," a jovial female voice ordered over his left shoulder. "It contains all the basic grains."

The scent of Shea's perfume tantalized him even before he swiveled his head. She looked down at him and his uneaten cereal with a sly expression of satisfaction. *She knows I hate this stuff,* he noted as he said, "Grain is for horses."

"Hmmm. Don't stand up," she instructed as he and the other two men started to their feet. "I can't stay very long." For one instant her slender, strong hand rested on Duke's shoulder, urging him to remain seated. He settled back in his chair and wondered how her touch could be so affecting on a neutral area like his shoulder. He'd stayed away from her the past two days, letting her mull over what had happened between them in his cottage. Staying away had done nothing but make him crave the sight of her, the scent, the sound of her voice.

"So you don't like the cereal," Shea noted. "Can I tell the waiter to bring you some poached quail eggs instead?" Her eyes beamed with challenge meant only for him to see.

"Nope. I like my eggs scrambled."

"I can arrange that."

Duke wanted to shoot back a risqué remark, but he squelched the urge. "Thanks," he answered primly. He swept a gaze over her short linen dress and matching white jacket. Red costume jewelry accented the outfit, and her hair was smoothed back in a neat French braid with a red bow at the back. She looked fantastic, like an ad from *Vogue*.

"You look too clean," he told her with a mischievous smile. "Like a . . . yeah, like a palomino all fixed up to go in the show ring. How can you stay so perfect and get any work done, Palomino?"

"You'll be happy to know that I'll be performing real work this afternoon," she answered. "One of our regular massage therapists had to fly home because her mother's sick, so I'm taking her clients."

"Which therapist?" Chip Greeson asked.

"Marly."

"Damn," Chip blurted. "She's my favorite, and I had a two-thirty appointment. Whoops. Sorry, Shea, I'm sure you're wonderful too."

Shea held up her hands. "Every finger full of poetry," she deadpanned. She looked down at Duke again, and he met her self-assured violet eyes with a wink.

"Well, have a good breakfast, everyone. Mr. Araiza, your cereal is getting soggy. Shall I have your waiter bring a fresh bowl?"

"Nope. I like whole-grain mush."

Her mouth quirking in an involuntary smile, she glided away. Duke watched her as she moved among the tables in the large room, smiling, greeting other diners. His body hardened at the thought of the taut curves and fragrant skin concealed by her dress jacket. Hell, the outfit made her sexier; it added to a mystique that he couldn't quite analyze. She carried herself regally, and Duke decided that the next palomino filly born on his ranch would be named Lady Shea in her honor. After she disappeared through a scalloped archway, he turned toward Chip.

"I'll trade you five candy bars for your massage appointment this afternoon," Duke told him.

A huge smile spread over Chip's face. "It's a deal."

The afternoon schedule for mud baths and massages was light; many of the guests were attending a Neiman Marcus fashion show in the estate's main ballroom. Shea finished a massage on Dame Lydia McCall, an aging British character actress. Dame Lydia, her stately and rather large body swaddled in a white guest robe, her high-pitched voice breaking into yawns even as she tried to tell Shea one more old show-girl story, padded into a small solarium and lay down on a lounge chair for a nap.

The other two massage therapists were busy with their clients, so Shea sat down in the reception area and idly waited for Chip Greeson to arrive. She was thumbing through a magazine and thinking about Duke Araiza when Duke's deep, melodic voice interrupted her.

"Massage me. Cover me in mud. I surrender." He stood in the doorway, arms outstretched, a martyred expression on his face.

Shea inhaled in soft, silent appreciation. Would the mere sight of him always make her feel as if she were floating? "Pardon me," she said after a moment, "but I take no prisoners without appointments."

"I have one. I bartered for it. Chip Greeson's."

She stood, eyeing him ruefully. Somehow she wasn't the least bit surprised at this turn of events. "And what did you—"

"Gold. Emeralds. Candy bars. Chip couldn't resist." Duke lowered his arms and hooked his thumbs over the elastic top of his sweatpants. He ambled toward her, his stride relaxed, the clingy pants revealing a universe of masculine delights. His eyes held a challenge. "I've been letting you simmer for the past two days. I had to force myself to leave you alone, and it's made me tense. I need a mud bath and massage. So what do I do first?"

Shea silently admitted that she was glad to see him, but she was through letting him have the upper hand. Duke Araiza would get very special treatment today. A little mild revenge would make her feel more in control.

"First you go into the men's locker room and take off all your clothes," she told him in a polite, serious tone. Shea handed him a key to one of the lockers. "You'll find a pair of one-size-fits-all shorts in your locker. You can wear those until I get you covered with mud, then pull them off. Follow the signs to mud room D. I'll be waiting there."

"Nice," he said, tipping his head toward her. She wore white sneakers, tailored white shorts, and a green golf shirt with a small emblem of the estate's coat of arms on the breast pocket. His eyes wandered over her. "I haven't really seen your legs all the way up before. I thought running only produced such wonderful results in horses."

"Thanks. I like being compared to a horse."

"Great fetlocks. Great knees. Great—"

"Your mud bath is waiting, sir."

Smiling, he strode off to the men's locker room. Shea ran to mud room D, where everything had been made ready for Chip Greeson. The room was soothingly warm, and brass wall sconces provided low, relaxed lighting. A white claw-footed tub, half-filled with creamy, mineral-rich mud, sat in the middle of the tiled floor. Six copper pails packed with mud sat beside the tub.

Shea stood there, waiting, hoping that she looked calmer than she felt. A minute later Duke appeared in the doorway. Her heart crept up under her collarbones and stayed there. Where were his shorts?

He had wrapped a small white towel around his hips, and it barely covered him. The ends didn't really meet; Duke held them together with one hand over his hip. The towel parted over his outstretched leg, revealing his thigh all the way to the hipbone.

"There weren't any shorts in my locker," he said solemnly. "I'm not lying. Really."

Shea didn't know how she managed to remain still and look undisturbed, but she credited the discipline to years of athletic pursuits. If she could push herself to run a fast mile, then she could deal calmly with Duke Araiza even though he was only wearing a hand towel.

"Get in the tub, please," she instructed.

He walked across the room slowly, with the kind of confident bearing that told her he'd never been shy about his body. Shea looked straight at him, but refused to let her eyes wander into the towel's vicinity. If anything moved underneath it and she saw it move, and Duke saw her see it move . . . the mood would definitely become more dangerous. She'd already gotten more danger than she'd bargained for.

"Couldn't find a larger towel, eh?" she asked as he stepped into the tub.

"Why, it would be like putting a rain coat on a Greek statue."

"Vanity, thy name is Araiza."

Shea watched, nearly hypnotized despite herself, as he eased down in the mud. The symmetry of his back muscles, which flexed as he settled into the tub, was pure male perfection. He leaned back, worked the towel free, and laid it across his lap. Duke Araiza, naked except for that small square of white cotton . . .

"Oink," he said gruffly.

Chuckling, Shea emptied the buckets of mud on top of his torso and legs, then silently reproached herself for feeling regretful when his magnificent body was hidden from view. *Revenge*, she recalled.

"Now what?" he asked, smiling wickedly. He pulled his towel out of the mud and dropped it on the floor. "Naked and ready."

"Now you put your head back, close your eyes, and I'll massage your face and scalp." She patted the black satin pillow attached to the rim of the tub.

Duke rested his head on the pillow and shut his eyes blissfully. "*Magnifico, querida*," he whispered.

Shea spent a wistful moment studying his angular, handsome features. Then she clenched her teeth, smiled grimly, and hoisted a remaining bucket of mud.

"You deserve this, *hombre*," she said fiendishly, and dumped the mud onto his head.

He sat up hurriedly, made a garbled shouting sound, sputtered, and grabbed for her with both big hands. Shea whooped with glee and darted back, but not far enough. He caught her by one wrist. "Take a wallow with me, hellion!"

"*Por favor! Por favor!* Please! No!" she yelped one second before he pulled her into the tub.

Shea flailed at his iron grip and began laughing as she sank into the mud between his updrawn knees. He shook his head, slinging mud everywhere like a dog shaking rainwater from its coat, and used his free hand to wipe his eyes.

"Ever think of starring in a remake of *The Jazz Singer?*" Shea managed to ask. She laughed harder. As a matter of fact she couldn't remember when she'd ever laughed this way. She couldn't remember when she'd sat in a tub full of mud with a naked man. Never, actually. He uttered a stream of colorful curses in Spanish and English.

"I see the whites of your eyes and the whites of your teeth," she continued. "But otherwise you look like a giant piece of chocolate. Like one of those giant chocolate Easter rabbits . . ."

"You play hard, *querida*. All right, I like that," he said in a tone that was half angry and half amused. "I deserved this."

"Yes, you did," she said in a voice gone suddenly soft. "And I enjoyed it immensely."

"But it won't be forgotten! You've toyed with a master gamesman! You've thrown down a challenge. . . ."

"Quiet, *hombre*," she ordered, and kissed him.

He went still for a second, and then his muddy arms went around her in a snug, possessive hold. Mud seemed to be everywhere except their mouths.

Shea wrapped both arms around his neck and burrowed as close as she could, kissing him wildly, giddy and thoughtless of everything except his taste and touch. She hadn't intended to kiss him, but her good intentions no longer mattered. He was outrageous, sexy, and a very good sport, three qualities that she admired tremendously. With a hoarse cry Duke twisted his mouth against hers. The kiss was wanton and yet something much more; they were equals, sharing a passion that encompassed respect and affection as well as hearty lust.

Mud slipped over the side of the tub as he squeezed her closer to him. Shea realized that she was lying between Duke's long, muscular legs, then that he had wrapped his legs around her. It was a strange feeling, to be wrapped in his body. It was a secure feeling.

Shea ran a hand up the back of his head. "Your hair, your poor muddy hair," she said between kisses.

"I'll go through a mud bath ten times a day if this kind of treatment comes with it," he replied hoarsely. He dipped his head and kissed a clean spot on her neck. "Hell, you're not really sorry about my hair. You're enjoying every second of what you did to me. You enjoy being reckless and bawdy. I knew those urges were hidden under that golden princess exterior of yours."

She sighed in a way that acknowledged that truth. "Oh, Alejandro, this is ridiculous and wonderful and—"

"Alejandro?" he repeated softly.

Shea wiped mud from his face and nodded sheepishly. "Do you mind? I think it's a wonderful name."

He smiled, his teeth looking so white against the mud-stained background of his face that she laughed again. He laughed too, then. "No one else calls me Alejandro. If you want to, that makes it special."

"It is special. You're special. If you weren't, I wouldn't be sitting in this tub of mud with you. I wouldn't have kissed you." She looked a little concerned. "I don't know what's going to happen between us, but—"

"Sssh. A very famous philosopher once said, *Que sera, sera*. What will be, will be."

"Famous philosopher, my foot. That was Doris Day," Shea retorted, chuckling.

"Yeah, so, but Doris was right." He was smiling at her, but slowly the smile faded, replaced by a look that was hungry and serious.

"I don't want to lose you," she whispered.

"Lose me?" he asked in a soft, worried voice. "No way."

"I'm not very good at relationships."

"But what about your friend?" Duke spoke gently. "The one who was killed."

Shea shook her head. "We weren't . . . like this. There was more friendship than passion." She laid one hand alongside Duke's jaw, as if to reassure both him and herself as she looked into his dark, sympathetic eyes. "I grew up lonely, Alejandro. No father, and a mother who had too many problems to spend much time caring what happened to me. I've learned to keep people at a distance so if they don't care about me, it won't hurt."

"Oh, *querida*," he said huskily, "I care about you, and I'll try not to hurt you."

Shea kissed him again, and her torso sank lower into the mud. Her stomach met his, and even the mud couldn't obscure the hard ridge of his aroused body. She nearly groaned at the open, ready feeling that surged through her own body in response.

"Part of me wants to make love to you right here," Shea whispered against his mouth. "And part of me— mostly the estate manager part—wants to vamoose before anyone sees us."

He took a deep breath, and she knew that he was

trying to calm his own impulses. For her sake, he was trying. And suddenly Shea knew just how easy it was to fall in love with him.

"*Querida*, there's all the time in the world," he whispered. Smiling stoically he planted a kiss on her nose.

"Alejandro, I don't think it would be a good idea if I gave you a massage today." Shea hugged him in apology. "Things are happening so fast, and that would only make them move faster. I'll get one of the others to . . ."

"No. It's all right." He nuzzled her ear. "I don't want anyone's hands on me but yours. I'll wait."

She had never really felt special to anyone. The feeling now, of being so special to Duke that he didn't want anyone else to touch him, made tears rise in her eyes.

She hugged him fiercely, then pushed herself back from him, but he trailed his hands along her arms and grasped both her hands. They faced each other in the tub full of mud. Shea looked down at herself, at her clothes covered in mud, at the stuff all over her arms. She looked at Duke, who still resembled a chocolate confection. They shared quirky little smiles that quickly grew into chuckles and then into full-fledged laughter.

Being a manager came naturally to Shea, and she assumed that it was both an inborn trait and a survival technique learned during her childhood. By the time she was ten years old she had taken charge of the household bills—when her mother had enough money to pay them. When there was no money, Shea became adept at sidetracking creditors. By the time she was twelve, she knew how to make her voice sound like an adult's when she spoke to bill collectors on the phone.

So now she felt certain that she could manage Duke.

He seemed to be mellowing on the subject of the estate. He had made friends with Chip Greeson and Glenda Farrar. He had actually attended a yoga class, though someone told her later that he fell asleep in the middle of meditation. His mantra was *steak*.

Shea checked the cheese-and-cauliflower casserole bubbling in her kitchen oven. Tonight Alejandro would eat health food and love it. She would bring him one step closer to appreciating her lifestyle and the estate.

When he arrived, he gave her oversize white T-shirt and snug white jeans a devilish once over, then kissed her firmly on the mouth. In return Shea deliberately scrutinized his short-sleeved print shirt, jeans, and loafers with no socks, then kissed *him* firmly on the mouth.

"White wine," he said grandly, and held out two bottles. "From a local vineyard."

She took it, nodding her thanks while she sighed inwardly. Guests weren't supposed to go traipsing off the estate grounds and buy wine. But she was determined to make tonight a peaceful interlude. "A little white wine never hurt anybody," she told him. "Wine is not incompatible with a healthy regimen."

"I'm so glad you approve," Duke told her indulgently, and made a low bow.

Shea laughed. "You don't care if I approve or not. You want to corrupt me."

"Yeah, but you're corrupting me too. I'd drink beer otherwise."

He followed her toward an immaculate little kitchen, gazing around the cottage as he did. Through a door in one corner he saw her bedroom, and Duke noted that its atmosphere was decidedly sensual—lacy pillows and a plush, satiny bedspread. She had a huge antique bedstead with roses carved into the head and footboard. *Roses. Appropriate*, Duke thought with a smile.

He could smell her roses-and-cream fragrance throughout the cottage.

The dining room and den of the small dwelling were filled with sleek, modern furniture. Pastel abstracts adorned the walls, and fat white pillows nestled on a fat white couch in front of a conical, freestanding fireplace. Bookcases held a collection of handmade ceramic vases. The bedroom floor was covered in creamy, thick carpet, but the rest of the cottage floors were shellacked hardwood dotted with rugs done in muted pastel colors.

"This place is as pretty and light as the inside of a flower," he remarked as she poured wine into two crystal goblets.

"And you're my invading bee," Shea teased.

His dark eyes sparkled as he flashed her a sexy smile. "Bzzzzz."

They ate at a small dining-room table decorated with a low glass dish in which tea roses floated in water. Besides the casserole, Shea had fixed bell peppers stuffed with rice and tofu, chicken covered in a light honey-and-sesame-seed glaze, homemade wheat bread, and kiwi fruit for dessert.

"I can live on it," Duke observed with an appreciative nod as he finished a bit of kiwi.

Her voice was droll. "Why, thank you."

"It's great, Shea. *Bueno.* I don't deny it. I wouldn't mind trading real food for it every once in a while, though." They sipped a second glass of wine and he continued, "There's something I have to know about you. Something very intimate."

"No more palm reading," she warned.

Duke chuckled. "Nope. It's about roses. You're a rose freak, *querida.* Your perfume, your bedstead, your table decorations, the rose bushes outside this house. There must be a story. I have to know."

Shea cleared her throat and looked down at her dessert plate, smiling tentatively and trying to ignore the pensive feeling that grew inside her. "I didn't realize you noticed so much about me." *As if I didn't notice everything about you, Alejandro. The careful way you hold delicate things, like the wine glass. The way the light shines on that black hair of yours. The way you bring life and vitality into my home.*

"I notice," he said simply. They looked at each other for several seconds, trading silent promises that they might someday fulfill together. "Tell me about the roses," he urged.

A memory came back to Shea so clearly that she could almost smell the stained city air and feel the sweaty heat of that Los Angeles day many years ago. And the roses. She would never forget the way they struggled valiantly amid the squalor. *Keep them alive for me, niño. This life, it is ugly, but the roses will always bring you love and beauty.* Those were the last words from Señora Savaiano's thin, ancient lips before the paramedics took her to the hospital for the last time. Shea had never forgotten the words or the flowers.

"A neighbor who took care of me when I was growing up loved roses," she told Duke slowly. "She managed to keep bushes of them growing outside the door to the apartments where my mother and I lived. Nothing else was beautiful about the place but those roses."

"The woman who took care of you?" he asked.

"My mother worked nights." Shea stood up. She cleared her throat, feeling uncomfortable, as usual, about discussing her past. "She was a waitress." *Discussion closed.* "Let's get the other bottle of wine and go into the living room."

"*Whoa!*" Duke exclaimed in dismay. "You always throw

out bits and pieces about your past, and then you clam up."

Shea walked around the table and stopped beside him, looking down at him with a taut frown on her face. Duke would allow no secrets between them; that both excited and frightened her. "My mother was a waitress," she repeated in a blunt, defensive tone. "We didn't have much money. Everything I have today—my education, my job, this place—I worked hard as hell to get. I hate to disappoint you, but I don't come from the classy background you assume. That's why I don't like to talk about the past."

He studied her for a moment, anger slowly etching itself into his features. *Dear Lord, but he could look fierce when he wanted,* Shea thought raggedly.

"Dammit!" he exploded. Duke stood quickly and caught her by one wrist, not painfully, but firmly. "Do you think I'm looking for a blond, debutante, society type to show off back home? So everyone will know that the grandson of a dirt-poor immigrant has really made good? Is that what you think?"

Shea tried to jerk her wrist out of his grip. "No! I'm not capable of that brand of snobbery, and I never will be! I just don't want you to have any foolish illusions! I'm a mustang!"

"A what?" he said in consternation, his brow furrowed.

Shea thought grimly that she must have sounded like an idiot. She repeated in a lower voice, "A mustang, at heart. Like you. Tough and mean and strong."

After a thoughtful moment he exhaled, his anger gone, and said, "Well, hell, I know that you're tough and mean and strong. What other kind of woman would dump a damned bucket of mud on my head?"

"Whatever you think of me, don't ever think that I look down on your background or your Mexican heritage. That's ridiculous. I grew up in a Los Angeles neighborhood that was more Mexican then American. I spoke Spanish almost as early as English."

He studied her, and after a moment his expression softened. He spoke gruffly. "You say you're a mustang. But you've got class too. And style. And compassion. And intelligence. And—"

"Enough, Alejandro, enough. You're embarrassing me."

"Somebody needs to embarrass you. Somebody needs to rattle your cage, and I'm the man to do it."

Without another word he grabbed her, swung her up into his arms, and marched into the living room. Stunned, Shea stared at his expression of determination as he strode to the couch. He dumped her unceremoniously on the soft cushions, then jabbed one blunt finger at her.

"I'll be right back with the other bottle of wine," he said in a firm tone. "Have you got a deck of cards?"

"Yes," she said, and pointed to a drawer at the bottom of the bookcases.

"Get it. Clear off your coffee table. I'll teach you how to play poker."

"I know how to play poker. I also know how to shoot craps."

He gave her a long, respectful look. "Good, Ms. Mustang. I'm not in the mood to shoot craps, if you don't mind."

"Me neither. We can play cards." She felt giddy and confused.

"Marvelous. Playing poker's one of the best ways to calm my nerves."

"Poor man," she commented dryly.

"*One* of the best ways, I said."

"I'm sorry for upsetting you a minute ago. I never meant to imply . . ."

"I'm a little oversensitive—comes from being treated like a second-class citizen when I was young." His voice became sardonic. "I guess we Latin types are bound to be temperamental."

"Me too. I'm not Latin, but I'm a temperamental something."

"Woman," he concluded for her. "All women are temperamental."

She threw a pillow at him as he made his way to the kitchen, and he threw it back. By the time he returned with the wine bottle and two fresh glasses, she was seated cross-legged on the floor, shuffling the cards atop her coffee table.

"That's better," he noted in a tone of grand satisfaction. "You've calmed down."

"Sit down and be quiet, *hombre*," she warned. "What are we playing? Five-card draw?"

"Fine." He took the deck.

"What are we betting, Alejandro? I don't have any chips, pennies, or matches."

"Let's improvise. No ante. Straight and simple. We'll bet clothes." When she arched one brow and gazed at him without speaking, he added, "Chicken?"

"I won't bet chickens. It isn't humane, and they'll drop feathers everywhere."

"Very cute."

"All right, Araiza, I'll play strip poker with you. I'm a shark, I warn you."

"I thought you were a mustang."

"Deal the cards, wise guy."

"My shirt against your shirt."

"Hah! Great! I'd love to have a man's shirt to sleep in."

"I'll use yours for a sweat rag."

"You're a cruel man, Alejandro." She smiled fiendishly and began dealing the cards.

When they both had a full hand, she nodded to him. "You first."

He laid his hand down. "Two pair."

Shea's eyes gleamed as she put her own cards on the table. "Three of a kind. Fork over the shirt."

Duke took a deep swallow from the wine glass beside his cards, then quickly unbuttoned his short-sleeved print shirt and pulled it off.

"I like this," Shea told him as he handed it across the coffee table. "The tiny black stripe in it is the color of your hair and eyes. I'll always think of you when I wear it. *Gracias.*"

"*De nada.* Your shirt against my pants."

"Brave man." Shea gloated until she put down a miserable pair in the next hand and he slapped down a straight.

"Your shirt, if you please," he ordered.

Shea was suddenly very glad she'd worn a bra under the light T-shirt with its colorful, hand-painted design. Grimacing because the shirt was a favorite of hers, she pulled it over her head and tossed it to him. He held it to his nose and inhaled deeply.

"Ah, roses and cream," he murmured gleefully. "I'll always think of you when I wipe my underarms with this."

"How wonderful."

They faced each other for an awkward moment, her eyes roving over his thickly haired chest, his taking in her rather demure white bra. "You shouldn't be wearing that," he complained solemnly. "It's bad for your lungs—makes it harder for your chest to expand when you breathe. Why don't you take if off?"

"Your theory about underwear is interesting but unproven," she told him in a wry tone.

"Let's prove it, then. Your bra against my jeans."

She shook her head. "My jeans against your jeans. I think my lungs are doing just fine for the time being."

"So be it. I'm a patient man."

When she laid down four of a kind in the next hand, Duke simply threw his cards on the table and groaned. "It's your lucky night," he grumbled, and began undoing his jeans.

Shea swallowed with difficulty and sat in rigid silence, wondering just what brand of insanity she'd created. Duke kicked off his loafers, shoved his jeans to his ankles, then held up each bare foot as he finished the duty. He folded the jeans carefully and presented them to her. The coffee table hid his lower half.

"Have you got anything left to bet?" she asked with more courage than she felt.

He arched one brow at her. "Just my briefs." He nodded toward her bra. "My briefs for your bra. You owe me one chance to win back my dignity. Come on, one more hand."

"I wasn't aware that a bra equaled dignity."

Duke smiled languorously. "It'll do."

Her heart pounding, she murmured a word of agreement. One more hand. He dealt the cards, and when Shea had all hers, she bent her forehead to the table and tossed them down. "Nothing," she mumbled. "I don't have anything." She heard his low chuckle.

"And I have three of a kind."

Shea raised her chin slightly and peered up at him. "What will you do with it? My bra?"

"Put it under my pillow for good luck. Or hang it from the antenna of the Ferrari."

"You wouldn't!"

"Give it here, *querida*. We're both honorable people, and a bet's a bet."

His eyes were too gentle for her to feel very embarrassed. Besides, Shea reminded herself, he'd seen her breasts before. She sat stiffly erect, trying to ignore the thudding of her pulse and the languid heat inside her. She had never before behaved this way. He seemed to sense her amazement.

"It's only a game," he said softly. "You don't have to go on. I don't want you to resent me or feel awkward."

Shea absorbed his concern, and all her resistance went slack. Her maverick rancher was the dearest kind of man. "I want to do it," she whispered. With one swift, quick movement, Shea reached behind her and undid the garment. Her chin up, she slipped the bra off and handed it to Duke with a formal little gesture of her hand.

He grasped her hand and his prize, then bent his head and nibbled her fingers. "You lose with grace," he said in a low, husky voice. "It's a sign of great character."

Shea withdrew her hand and sat very still, looking straight at his dark eyes. They flickered down to her exposed breasts, and he smiled in such a tender way that she smiled back.

"All my life," he said softly, "I've been waiting for you. Rich girl, poor girl, debutante, waitress's daughter—whatever you are or were doesn't matter. I don't care about those things. I love the way you talk back to me. I love your gracefulness. I love the way you care about this silly place and its guests. And I think you're the most beautiful woman I've ever seen."

Shea exhaled a long, trembling breath. "Oh, Alejandro, you make it very easy to forget. Today in the mud bath, it was *so* easy. And now." She pulled a pillow from the couch behind her and, turning toward him again, lightly hugged it to her breasts. It made her feel less vulnerable.

"Forget what?" he asked, puzzled.

Her voice held sorrow, not rebuke. "That you own this estate and might decide to change everything about it. This place is my life. To you it's just something you won in a game. Can't you leave it as is and be happy with the money it makes for you?"

After a moment his eyes darkened with regret, and he shook his head slowly. "No, *querida*, I can't leave it alone. No more than I can leave you alone."

"It's not the elegance that bothers you," she said in a low, even tone, "it's the serenity. You can't believe that life is supposed to be calm and pleasant. You're only happy when life is difficult and chaotic, because that's the way you grew up."

"Life should include both good and bad qualities. One makes you appreciate the other."

Shea's expression was grim. "I know all about difficulty and chaos. I grew up with them, the same way you did. That's precisely why I *do* appreciate the estate. I left the bad things behind when I came here."

"You've run too far," he said in a worried tone. "You've cut yourself off from the real world too much."

"This *is* the real world."

They gazed at each other wistfully, both realizing that they had reached an impasse. "I don't want this argument to ruin what's happening between you and me," he told her quietly. "Whatever I do with the estate, I'll take care of you."

Shea could feel her face flame red. She handed him his jeans and shirt. "I don't need for anyone to take care of me. I've taken care of myself almost all my life."

He nodded, looking a little angry. "That's the problem, *querida*. I understand, because I used to feel the same way. But it's not a good way to lead a life. You have to learn that. You have to learn to accept as much pleasure as you give."

When she didn't answer, he knew that she agreed with him, but was too proud to admit it. Duke dressed quickly, aware as he did that she watched him sadly, and that her wide violet eyes glistened with tears. Lithe and flexible for such a tall man, he crossed to her side of the table and knelt down beside her. He pressed her bra back into her hand. Then he met her eyes and the sorrow in them tore him up inside. Someday he would ease her beyond the superficial details of her past and learn what traumas had given her such sorrow and such strength.

"Sleep well, *querida*," he whispered. "We'll figure all this out. Don't worry."

She leaned forward and kissed him, her mouth giving friendship and apology and farewell. Duke inhaled the scent of her perfume mingled with her own body. He nearly groaned with frustration that was both sexual and emotional. If he didn't go back to his own cottage immediately, he'd succumb to a dangerous impulse to just give her the estate, thereby removing the obstacle that kept her out of his arms. But the estate was too important to his future plans.

He had faith that Shea—compassionate, tenderhearted Shea—would trust him when she learned what he'd decided to do.

Five

Three days later one of the estate's staff members found Glenda Farrar sobbing uncontrollably in the Japanese garden. Shea listened anxiously as the staffer described the situation from a telephone in Glenda's room. Glenda was in bed. She wouldn't elaborate on her problems; besides being near hysterics she'd broken out in hives.

The estate kept two physicians on duty to advise guests on specific health problems, and Shea accompanied one of them to Glenda's room. After the doctor left, Shea sat on the edge of the bed and held her hand. Glenda looked small and round under the satin coverlet, and her face was still swollen from crying.

"Glenda, I have to know if anyone on the staff did something to upset you," Shea asked in a soothing tone.

"Oh, no, honey, that's not it at all!" Glenda's lower lip trembled. "It's p-personal. So . . . embarrassing."

Shea squeezed her hand. "Then consider me a friend you can trust. If I can help, tell me the problem."

"You can't h-help. It concerns Dan Steinberg." Her face crinkled while she held back new tears.

71

Shea ached as she watched the matronly little woman. "You've had an argument with him?"

"Oh, no! I never have arguments. They give me head-aches. I . . . I've never been very assertive, you see. Not with my first husband, rest his soul, or my children, or even with the customers in my boutique. I have a manager who handles customer complaints."

"Then what . . ."

"Oh, this is so humiliating." She began to cry softly. "I attempted to seduce Dan last night, and he rejected me."

"Ah," Shea said, trying in vain to picture Glenda trying to seduce someone.

"I put on a negligee and my best robe, and I went to his room. I told him that a w-woman has to be frank about these things. He said that a man has to be f-frank too. He was so awfully polite. So kind." She covered her face with both hands and sobbed. "I'll never look him in the eyes again!"

Shea tried to think of some positive aspect to the situation. "Glenda, for a nonassertive person you certainly did a very assertive thing by going to Dan's room."

"I would never have had the courage if Duke hadn't coached me." Glenda wiped her face with a pink tissue embossed with the estate's emblem, then sank back on her bed pillows and smiled wanly. "Duke advised me at length on the proper way to get a man's attention." She looked at Shea wretchedly. "I don't think I can ever come back here. I might run into Dan again."

Shea felt slow fury begin to boil in her stomach. How could Duke have the callousness to send this delicate soul on such a traumatic mission?

Shea struggled to keep her voice low and soothing. "Glenda, everyone on the staff adores you. You're one of our favorite guests. Please promise me that you'll wait until you feel better before you make any decisions about not returning here."

"I promise," Glenda murmured. And then she began to cry again.

Shea found Duke in his cottage. When he came to the door, he held a portable telephone in one hand and a sheaf of papers in the other. His black hair was ruffled, making him appear more like a maverick and less like a businessman. He wore loose khaki shorts and a white undershirt that was snug on his broad chest. The white of the shirt accented the honeyed bronze of his skin and seemed to match his teeth when he smiled at her. A pair of wire-rimmed glasses were perched just above the fine white scar on his nose.

Shea stared at his glasses and Duke grinned. "I'm farsighted. Blind as a mole when it comes to reading."

Shea recaptured her composure. "I'd say the term is shortsighted," she told him grimly, thinking of Glenda Farrar. "May I come in?"

"Anytime, *querida*." Frowning at her tone of voice, he stepped aside and let her enter. He went to the desk and deposited his papers, then removed his glasses. "Running a horse-racing operation is a helluva complicated thing these days," he noted, gesturing toward the desk. "I feel like a corporate honcho sometimes. Good Lord, my attorneys have attorneys. That's how complex things are. Shea, you really can't blame me for missing another yoga class when I have so much work to do. I'm not here on vacation, you know." He eyed her green silk skirt and matching blouse. "*Exquisita.*"

"This has nothing to do with missed classes," she told him tautly, crossing her arms over her chest. "This has to do with Glenda Farrar." Shea briefly explained about Glenda's misery. "How could you?" she finished angrily. "Couldn't you see that she's painfully shy? You can't tell someone like that to march into a man's bedroom and offer an invitation. The rejection has devastated her! She may never come back to the estate!"

Shea noted that Duke's expression had grown dark while she spoke. Now his eyes were cold with reproach. "She asked for my advice. I gave it. She can't live in her fantasy world the rest of her life. No more than you can."

Shea clenched her fists together in frustration. "Her fantasy world is a safe place! Can't you understand that some people don't belong in your world? That it's too harsh for them?"

"For you?"

Shea shut her eyes and shook her head slowly. "I don't know, I don't know." She looked up at him again. "At least you could use more delicacy and diplomacy. Did you actually tell Glenda to seduce Steinberg?"

Duke sighed, his face still tense and his eyes smoldering. "I told her to give it a shot, yes. And if Steinberg were worth a damn, he'd have taken her up on the offer. I suspect that the guy's not straight."

"And how did you come to that conclusion?"

"Intuition. And he has a lousy handshake. Like a balloon with all the air let out."

"Oh, Alejandro!" she said in exasperation. "That's not a fair assessment."

"Do you want me to tell Glenda what I suspect about him? Maybe it'd make her feel better. I wouldn't deliberately do anything to hurt her . . . "

"No! Please leave counseling duties to someone on the staff. We try to cultivate a relaxed, happy attitude here. I can't have my guests upset."

"They're my guests too," he reminded her. "And I don't need anyone's permission to talk to them."

Shea absorbed his remark. As the blunt emotional impact hit, her energy drained away. "Least of all mine," she said in a low, deflated voice. Her shoulders slumped and she looked at him grimly. "I apologize." The angry set of his face softened and he took a step toward her, one hand reaching out. But she straightened her shoulders and shook her head. "I really do apologize," she said formally. "I keep forgetting that I'm your employee."

He winced. "I don't want you to feel that way, dammit."

"But I am, you see. And I'm not going to forget it again." She started toward the door.

"Don't walk out of here like that," he ordered in Spanish. Shea stopped as he came to her and grasped her shoulders. "We communicate more clearly when we don't speak English," he explained tersely. "Spanish is more emotional."

"*Sí*," she murmured, and in that language said to him, "Are you ordering me to stay as your employee? All right. If you're ordering me to stay as your woman, then I'm leaving."

"I don't need to talk to my employee," he said wearily, and let go of her.

She opened the door and left without another word.

Shea and several of the estate's staff members were drinking espresso after dinner at Jennie Cadishio's Mendocino home. Shea listened in gloomy silence as Alex, the weight-room manager, talked about an encounter he'd had with Duke.

"And so Mr. Araiza whispered to me, 'I'll bet you five bucks the big redheaded guy can't bench press more than two-fifty.' And I said, 'Mr. Araiza, Shea would kill me if I bet on a guest's performance in the weight room.' Mr. Araiza laughed and nodded.

'She's a dangerous woman,' he said, 'but that's the best kind.' "

Everyone at the table smiled at her, and Shea stared down into her cup, frowning. She'd never heard herself described as dangerous before, and neither had the staff.

"He's going to change everything, I'm afraid," she told them quietly. Shea glanced up and found that somber expressions had replaced their smiles. Jennie was looking at her in the wide-eyed way only Jennie could manage—stoical and scared at the same time. "I'm just trying to prepare you," Shea added. "I wish I could tell you what he has in mind, but I don't know yet myself."

"Will he close down the estate?" Jennie asked glumly.

"Somehow I don't think so. But who can predict? He might turn the chateau into a ranch house and put a herd of horses on the golf course."

"At least we wouldn't need to fertilize the greens anymore," someone noted.

Shea managed a smile. "I can tell you, *amigos*, that the new owner only appreciates tequila, women, and burritos."

"And we have to teach him to appreciate mineral water, celibacy, and alfalfa sprouts," Jennie noted wryly. "I think we should give up."

As everyone chuckled, Shea simply nodded.

The day's events had left her tired and in a bad mood, so she excused herself soon after dinner and headed back toward the estate. She eased her small, well-kept Honda along Highway 1, the winding coast road. From time to time she glimpsed the Pacific to her left. In the moonlight it churned and broke against craggy cliffs and beachless shores strewn with boulders.

The northern California coast was wild and vibrant, sometimes frightening but always exciting. Shea felt drawn to these wind-torn edges of the continent. She rubbed her forehead wearily and cursed under her breath. She was drawn toward the combination of rugged beauty and peril—the same qualities embodied in Alejandro Araiza.

The car slipped through the night, leaving the ocean view for a few minutes to delve into deep forest. Shea passed a roadside inn tucked into the apron of woodland, and a distracted part of her brain registered the fact that she'd glimpsed a red Ferrari in the crowded parking lot. The inn had a small bar and dance floor, making it a favorite hangout among the locals.

Shea jerked the Honda to a stop, backed up quickly, and drove into the inn's lot.

Inside, the bar was dark and opulent, with touches of Mendocino's Victorian style in the ornate woodwork and stained-glass lamps. The jukebox in one corner of the dance floor made a weird modern contrast to the surroundings. The bar's patrons were a mixture of tourist and local, young and old. At the moment many of them were dancing. On the jukebox Elvis sang "I Can't Help Falling in Love With You."

Duke spotted Shea at almost the same second that her intense violet gaze came to rest on him. He felt a jolt of energy surge through him as yearning and anger fought for control of his emotions, but he remained as he was, leaning nonchalantly against the bar. His hand tightened around a glass of beer as he noted that most of the men in the bar turned their heads to look at her, at the sleek symmetry of lithe body and unique face and shoulder-length blond hair.

She wore gray flats, gray leather pants, and a wide-necked blue top that slipped off one golden shoulder. *Come on, Palomino, come on*, he told her silently as she made her way through the crowd toward him. *Let's tangle, lady. Let's stop pretending that we can control this.* She returned his gaze with challenge, sweeping her eyes over his boots, jeans, and white knit pullover. Duke smiled at her undaunted attitude.

She stopped only inches from him.

"I went AWOL from the estate," he told her bluntly, confirming the accusation in her eyes. "Just for tonight."

"And you don't give a damn if you set a bad example."

"I've never tried to set a good example for anyone. Let's dance." *To hell with polite chitchat.*

He put his beer aside and quickly took her arm. She tried to pull away, but he resolutely dragged her onto the dance floor.

"Alejandro, this is ridiculous!" She spoke in Spanish, her voice low and full of tension. "Stop! I don't want to dance. I just stopped to tell you how I—"

"You're dancing. It's too late." He wrapped her in a tight embrace.

The sudden, unexpected closeness of their bodies silenced them both. Shea felt warm currents of sensual response flow through her. Her breasts were snug against his chest, her pelvis tight against his. She grasped his shoulders and the sheathed contours of his muscles moved beneath her hands like bands of flexible steel.

They danced without speaking, communicating their anger and sorrow through the rigid set of their bodies. His hands clasped her lower back with harsh pressure; she knotted her fingers in his thin sweater as if she wanted to shake him. Shea stared straight into his dark eyes, trying very hard and without success to unsettle the strength she saw there. The song ended and another began, Chicago's achingly sensual "Color My World." Shea shut her eyes and sagged a little. The song was Duke's ally.

"What will be, will be," he reminded her in a troubled and sardonic voice.

"If things were different."

"Sssh. Live in the moment."

Her hands knotted tighter in the material of his pullover, and she leaned her forehead against his shoulder. He hardened with arousal, and without thinking Shea pressed her stomach into that hardness. She tilted her head back and looked up into his face. His eyes were half-closed, sensual, compelling, with sadness gleaming in the dark depths. She had never shared such conflict and such need with another human being. A soft groan escaped from her throat.

He bent his head beside hers and brushed her ear with his lips. "You and me, Palomino. What's between us is all that's important. Nothing else. I won't let *any* problem drive you away from me."

His arms tightened around her and she felt him tremble. That vulnerable response made her bones melt. With another soft cry, Shea burrowed her face into the smooth, dark hollow of his neck and kissed the warm skin beneath his ear.

"Oh, Lord, I don't believe this," she murmured in a choked voice. "Thirty minutes ago I was at dinner in Mendocino, warning Jennie Cadishio and some of the other staffers about your intentions, and now here I am . . ."

"Where you belong. You worry too much." He drew his head back slightly and brushed his mouth over hers. They clung to each other, swaying in time with the song, and she began to cry very softly.

"If you hurt the estate, you hurt me, Alejandro. I want you to know this."

"Shea, *querida*, don't cry," he said in a husky voice as he stroked her cheek. "Whatever final decision I make, I won't change things so much. You'll still be happy with the estate. You can run it almost as you please. Forget your fears. Love me, *querida*. Love me."

Shea composed herself quickly and took a deep breath. "I don't want to fall in love with you," she said in torment. "We're too much alike, Alejandro. Both stubborn."

"I think you've already fallen in love with me," he said very softly. "As I have with you."

"People don't fall in love this way. Things like this don't happen to me. I don't trust what I'm feeling. I've never gotten much love. . . ."

"And I've never offered much love," he interjected. "So we have to practice. Together. The estate and its problems will take care of themselves."

They looked at each other, and Shea spoke words that she instantly regretted. "You're a betting man," she blurted. "Let's play poker for the estate."

His eyes hardened and he arched one brow at her. "You never give up. The estate's all that matters to you."

Shea looked at him sadly for several seconds. She'd hurt him without intending to. And it was too late to turn back. "If it belonged to me, then our problems would be solved. I'm not asking for a gift. I'm asking for a chance. You like to take chances."

His eyes narrowed as he assessed her, and she held his dark gaze calmly. "You're an amazing woman," he said in a low, thoughtful tone. "So determined to protect what you love. The estate, that is, not me."

"Alejandro," she began, her eyes troubled, but he cut her off tensely.

"And if we played poker for the estate, what would *you* bet of equal value?"

"I don't know—"

"A month," he interjected. "A month with me. Doing

whatever I ask you to do, going wherever I ask you to go with me. And sharing my bed, of course."

Shaking, Shea pushed herself away from him. "That's a despicable suggestion," she said in a low, fierce voice. "When I make love to a man, it won't be because he won me in a poker game."

"I never expected you to take me up on the suggestion." He let go of her as she took another step back. "I want both you *and* the estate," Duke told her bluntly. "And I'm patient."

Shea gave him another tormented, sorrowful look. "You want too much," she said hoarsely.

Duke simply shook his head. She turned and made her way toward the exit. His eyes never left her.

The next day after lunch Shea returned to her office to find Glenda waiting in the reception area. "I really *must* speak to you," she told Shea excitedly, smiling.

"Well, of course."

They went into the office and Jennie closed the door behind them. Glenda grasped Shea's hands. "It's the most amazing thing. I'm a new person."

Shea pointed to a settee by one window and they went to it. "You're feeling better?" she asked when they were seated.

"Yes! You know, I was in a horrible state the other day, but after my hives cleared up, I thought, 'Why, Glenda, you did do an amazing thing by going to Dan's room. You proved that you could be assertive and survive the consequences.' "

When Shea didn't comment, she added, "It's just as Duke said. You must try something, he said, and if it goes wrong, then you must try something else. But you must never blame yourself for failing, when you've done your best." She smiled. "I still feel embarrassed that Dan refused my . . . uhmmm . . . advances, but I'm elated that I had the . . . the guts to give it a shot! Duke was so right!"

Shea leaned back on the settee and shook her head numbly. "You're sure you feel better about the incident?"

"Why, my dear, I feel better about my whole life!"

After Glenda left the office, still bubbling about how wonderful Duke's advice had been, Shea sat back down and pressed her hands to her face. "Okay, Somerton," she said aloud, "you misjudged him. He's right about Glenda Farrar. What else is he right about?"

She went to the intercom and called Jennie. "Check Duke Araiza's schedule for the afternoon and tell me where he is, please."

"He's gone riding. I sat at his table during lunch. Overheard him tell Chip Greeson that he needed to 'clear the cactus out of his mind,' so he was going for a long ride. A man who looks like Duke Araiza shouldn't be out in the woods alone. A female Bigfoot might carry him off."

Shea thought firmly, *Not if I carry him off first.* To Jennie she said, "Call the stable and have someone saddle a horse for me."

Of course, Duke wouldn't stick to the marked trails, Shea mused with grim humor as she guided her stocky gray gelding up an incline flanked on both sides by deep forest. Being a maverick and an expert horseman, he'd explore territory where other guests would never dare venture. She was startled by how well she knew him, a man she'd met less than two weeks ago. Deep, unshakable intuition told her where he might be found.

A narrow deer trail branched off to the right, winding through the forest like a temptation to leave safety behind. Shea's horse followed it until they entered a grove of large redwoods, where the silence deepened and the light grew shadowy. The forest floor was clear of underbrush and the big trees stood like monuments in a well-kept park.

When they reached a boulder beside the trail, Shea turned her horse left and urged him up a hill so steep that she had to lean forward to keep her balance in the saddle. They topped the hill and followed a ridge for several minutes. The forest parted and Shea reined her horse to a stop.

An old gazebo stood in the center of a small, grassy clearing. Spring water trickled from a pipe on the far side and made a slender channel that disappeared into the forest. Grape vines draped the gazebo in festive greenery, and flowers surrounded the little structure.

Duke straightened beside the spring pipe, water seeping unnoticed from his cupped hands, his dark eyes studying her calmly. It was as if he'd expected her.

Leading her horse behind her, Shea walked toward Duke. His shirt lay across the gazebo's railing; he wore only jeans and boots. His face and torso glistened where he'd recently splashed water on himself. A large black gelding, its gear removed, was tied to a tree at the other side of the clearing. The trail horses always wore halters and tie ropes under their bridles.

"I suspected that you'd find this place," she told him quietly as she came to a stop in front of him. "Somehow I *knew*."

"You come here too, then." His voice was low and husky. "I thought so." He pointed toward a patch of shrubbery by the steps to the gazebo. "Roses."

"I planted them."

"I figured. Did you put the gazebo here?"

"No. I came across it one day when I was exploring. It must have been built by the person who owned the estate before Sir Nigel. It needed repairs, but I didn't want anyone else to know about it, so I lugged paint and materials up here and fixed it myself." She smiled self-deprecatingly. "Don't study it too closely. I'm a terrible carpenter."

"Looks like the work was lovingly done." His eyes were troubled, but respect flickered in their depths. "This is your special spot. I'll be going."

Shea shook her head slowly. "No. I came to find you. To apologize."

"Hmmm. Is that so?"

"I'm sorry for saying that you had no delicacy or diplomacy when you gave advice to Glenda Farrar." She briefly related her conversation with Glenda. "You helped her. I was wrong. What you told her to do was very wise." Shea looked away, a little embarrassed. "I'll trust your intuition more, after this."

He put one hand under her chin and turned her face toward his. "Maybe I'll be more careful with my advice to our guests," he promised.

Our guests. She smiled tentatively. "Maybe the estate would benefit more if I worked with you instead of against you."

His eyes gleamed at that remark. "Stay," he urged in a soft voice. Duke nodded at their surroundings. "Enjoy the scenery."

"All right," she agreed just as softly. He took her horse and led it over to the side of his. Together they removed the gelding's gear, then tied the horse's lead to a sturdy sapling.

"There," Duke noted. "Now he'll be able to eat some grass, like my horse. They'll stay happy and quiet."

"It must be nice to be happy and quiet."

"It's an acquired skill. Come on, let's practice."

They walked back to the gazebo and sat down on the lowest step. Duke stretched his long legs out and leaned back, propping his elbows on the step behind him. Shea hugged her knees and inhaled the rich scent of the forest. It mingled with the musky fragrance of Duke's body, so close beside hers.

"I'm afraid," she whispered.

"What are you afraid of, Shea?"

She turned her head and gave him a bittersweet look. "That I'm going to make love to you regardless of what you do about the estate. That nothing's more important than being with you." She paused, shivering a little. "I'm not accustomed to feeling that way."

He sat up, then closed his eyes for a second, as if offering a silent prayer of gratitude. Afterward he looked at her with gentle mock rebuke. "I hope you haven't ever felt that way before. I want to be the first. And the last."

She wore jeans and a pink T-shirt. When he put one broad hand on the center of her back and stroked, it was as if she wore no shirt at all. Her skin burned from his caress.

"Come to me," he urged in a husky tone. Her soft moan told him that her last shred of resistance had just evaporated.

"Alejandro, my *hombre*."

She turned toward him, put her arms around his neck, and kissed him deeply. His skin felt hot under her hands; the whole world felt deliciously hot and promising as his tongue thrust into her mouth. He drew back, breathing roughly, and nodded toward the grass nearby.

"Now," he murmured, his eyes burning into hers.

Shea nodded. "Yes."

They lay down on the soft carpet, his arms around her, their legs entwined. Shea ran her hands over his bare chest with a greedy abandon she'd never felt before; he was all muscle and sun-baked skin, and his chest hair was a soft pelt that invited her fingers.

"Here. Touch me here. I've dreamed about you doing this to me." He put her hands on one of his flat brown nipples, and she smiled at him tenderly as she circled first it, then its twin, with her fingernail. He sighed. "You're even better than the dreams."

He removed her T-shirt and tossed it aside, then bent his head to kiss her lightly and repeatedly, skimming her mouth and face, then moving down to her neck, her shoulders, and the delicate skin above the cups of her bra. He savored her as if she were fine white chocolate, too wonderful to be consumed hurriedly.

She felt perspiration gathering on her skin. "You're burning me up inside," she said in a pleading tone. "And it's magnificent."

He whispered several earthy words of praise in Spanish, and her back arched as if he'd stroked her. Shea looked up into his eyes to find admiration there. "I just wanted to see if you'd understand those," he murmured, smiling tenderly.

"I didn't grow up sheltered, Alejandro. In my neighborhood, everyone knew those words."

"I meant them to be loving."

"I know," she answered, her eyes never leaving his. She cleared her throat and complimented him in the same frank, gentle way, using words she never thought she'd hear from her own lips. But they were right, because civilized words would never do justice to this lovely, rough-cut diamond of a man. And as she whispered them to him, his eyes glittered and his breath came faster.

"An amazing woman," he said at last.

They kissed again, and their hands traded explorations, sometimes slow, sometimes hurried, but always with a sense of wonder. He undid the fastenings that held her hair and ran his fingers through the rich golden strands, calling her Palomino as he did.

Shea trailed her fingertips down the center of his stomach and then to the coarse material of his jeans. He shuddered as she traced the outline of his desire beneath the fabric. When she cupped him, his hips moved reflexively. Chuckling between clenched teeth, he pulled her hand up to his mouth and kissed it.

"Whoa, *querida*. Control is too important, and I've almost lost mine."

She burrowed her head against his throat and licked the hollow of musky skin between his collarbones. "You're the man who's chided me for being too controlled."

"Ah, I remember. And I need to do something about that right now."

Abruptly he pushed her flat on her back and kissed her roughly, his tongue darting in and out of her mouth, his lips grinding on hers with a calculated force that aroused her without causing pain. He anchored both hands on the straps of her white bra and tugged it to her waist, then reached under her and jerked the snap free.

Shea gasped as he suddenly put his mouth on one of her nipples, his lips and tongue working in unison to delight her. He treated the other nipple just as well, then cupped her breasts in his hands and squeezed them rhythmically.

The world was falling away from her, lost in a haze of emotion and desire that cleansed her of lingering doubts. She had been waiting for this man all her life. She raised her head and watched the intimacy taking place between his mouth and her skin. Shea sighed with happiness and tried to talk, to be more than a languid participant in the beautiful drama that was unfolding, but he gently pressed one finger to her lips.

"Enjoy. Let yourself be pleasured. Let yourself be loved," he crooned.

Her head sank back, and she twined her fingers into his black hair. Her body was so heavy and limp that when he got on his knees and began removing her boots she wondered whimsically how he could lift her feet.

She watched, transfixed, as he undid her jeans and hooked his fingers into the waistband. With infinite care he stripped the last of her clothes away, then knelt beside her again, his eyes roaming over her slowly, as if her body were a map he wanted to memorize at first sight.

"*Exquisita,*" he told her gruffly. He put a hand on her flat, quivering, stomach and stroked downward to the golden curls between her thighs. Shea made small sounds of encouragement over the way his touch directed heat and tension to gather low in her body. She stiffened, trying not to lose control completely.

"Don't hold back," he whispered hoarsely. "Don't be a lady. Be *my* woman, and let your body show me how good my touch feels."

With a low moan of agreement, she arched to meet his gentle, provocative touch. With a suddenness that surprised them both, she shook wildly and tossed her head from side to side. Waves of pure bliss flowed through her, and dimly she heard his voice urging her on. He took her face between his hands and kissed her as she drew deep breaths.

When he sat back on his heels and began fumbling hurriedly with his jeans she raised up, her hair disheveled, her body trembling. "No!" she cried. "Let me. Please, Alejandro, let me."

He gave her a smile of muted frustration and great

tenderness, then stretched out on his back and shut his eyes tightly. His chest rose in a harsh, deep rhythm as she undressed him, and he clenched his hands into fists. Shea whispered words of praise as she revealed all of him to the summer day and her adoring eyes.

"You're not a mustang," she said, and her voice broke with the sweet agony of wanting him. "You're a Thoroughbred, inside and out, Alejandro. *Amante.*" The word meant "lover."

He moaned, then pulled her to him. She nestled by his side, her hand caressing his body lightly, almost in a soothing way when it embraced the hard, pulsing length of him. Duke knew that he should make an effort to cool his body down so that there would be no hurry, but he was too far gone. He called Shea's name and turned her to lay on her back again. He covered her with his body and she slipped both strong, golden legs around his hips. He braced himself over her and deliberately, desperately, kept himself from entering her.

"It's all right," she said in an urgent, loving tone. "It will be fast this time, Alejandro. We both know that. Don't suffer. Come here. Come here, sweetheart . . "

The endearment was more than his restraint could bear, and he thrust quickly into her warmth. She bathed him in the damp, tight secrets of her body, and he thrust again, harder. "Oh, *querida*, you feel wonderful," he said raspily. Duke forced himself to be still and savor the incredible welcome she had given him. He studied her violet eyes, afraid that the first moment had been too rough.

"You feel wonderful too," she told him breathlessly, and he relaxed. In her eyes he saw happiness and something more—a pure adoration that he'd never found in another woman's gaze.

He started carefully, using deep, slow movements to

test her reaction and the limits of his control. To his delight and amazement her body writhed and she tilted her head back, gasping in soft breaths. Her hands crept to his shoulder and held fiercely, as if she were afraid that she might fall off the edge of the world.

"Again?" she asked hoarsely, sounding surprised at her response. Then she smiled tremulously, mixed his name in a ragged moan, and whispered, "Oh, yes, again."

Tears stung Duke's eyes as he felt her pleasure released a second time, as it encompassed him and made him groan. He was strong and invincible; he knew that he could give this incredible woman as much happiness as she gave him.

He buried his face in her hair and let control slip away from him as he plunged into her with tender wildness. His arms snaked under her and clasped her tightly. She put her cheek against his face and urged him on with small sounds of delight. Shaken to the soul, burned and reborn a much better man than before, Duke called her name as his world exploded in sensation.

She held him possessively as their breathing slowed, and he would rather have died than leave the harbor of her body. He nuzzled the side of her neck, drew a trail of kisses upward, and touched his lips to her smile. She seemed to radiate light and joy as she looked up at him.

He wanted so badly to say that he loved her, but he thought the words might worry her. Duke winced inwardly with the effort of not revealing what he felt, but he forced himself to smile, to hide his inner struggle.

"I love you," she whispered. "There's absolutely no point in denying it any longer. And I don't want to deny it. I *love* you, Alejandro."

Duke stared down at her in amazement, wondering

if she could read his mind. Then he grasped her face between his hands. "It took courage to admit that," he murmured tenderly. "Now you have to let me love you in return,"

"I'll try, Alejandro, I'll really try."

With those heartfelt words as a promise, they hugged each other tightly.

Six

It was so good, better than meditation, even better than a runner's high, Shea admitted with a dreamy smile. And it was so simple. All she had to do was float here in Duke's private pool, her body enclosed in his strong, loving arms, her back against his broad chest. He sat on the pool's lowest step so that the water covered them both from the shoulders down. She lazed in his lap as if he were a luxurious masculine chair.

They'd made certain that the cottage's atmosphere was conducive to complete relaxation, with soft, slow music on the stereo system. The pool was shadowy, lit only by the light of a small lamp by the bed. Duke's warm breath touched her cheek and ear as he nuzzled her.

"Sleeping?" he asked softly.

"Hypnotized," she replied. He chuckled, and his hands returned to the job of stroking her stomach. His chest hair was a tickling, silky delight against her back, and his powerful thighs flexed under her as he shifted. Shea sighed happily. "Now I understand why guests pay such exorbitant amounts of money to rent the cottages that have pools," she admitted. "This feels fantastic. You feel fantastic."

His voice was devilish and seductive. "After last night, I was water-logged. But happy. Incredibly happy."

"We shouldn't have stayed in the pool for three hours."

"Ah, *querida*, but the time flew."

"Oh, yes." She twisted her head so that she could look up at him and smiled, for which she received a long, delicious kiss. His hand moved over her breasts, causing the water to undulate around them. He rubbed her nipples until he was satisfied that they could grow no harder. "Me too," she murmured in a haze of pleasure.

"Hmmm?"

"Incredibly happy. Me too." She stretched languidly as he ran one hand under her. "You're quite forward, sir," Shea teased. "Why, how dare you touch me there?"

He growled with comical lechery. "How about *there*?"

"That's even more impolite!" Shea slipped a hand behind her. "You see, *hombre*, I can be impolite too." Her breath paused in her throat as she gently grasped him. He was an amazing man, so tender and unhurried, but always so ready to make love to her.

"So this is the culprit," she whispered throatily while her fingers explored with wanton intent. "I wondered if perhaps a sea monster had gotten into your pool and was bumping me with its nose."

"It is a sea monster, and it's looking for a cave."

Chuckling, he sank a little and cupped his body further under hers. Shea quivered as the hard, smooth length of him nestled between her thighs.

When he hugged her, she tilted her head back in order to nuzzle his hair, then angled her hips so that it was impossible for their bodies to remain separate. With a quick movement, she surrounded him.

"Why, why, what kind of boy do you think I *am*?" he

protested in a low, rumbling voice. When she tantalized him by rolling her hips forward and back, he said huskily. "If you don't stop that, I think . . . I think I'll . . . smile."

Shea gasped as his body strained upwards, carrying heat and desire to her core. The time for teasing was past. "Alejandro," she whispered. "I need you so much. I need you again."

Groaning, he clasped her to him harshly, holding her as if she were a prisoner. With great care he took small bites at the back of her neck, and her legs writhed helplessly against his. "More," she begged.

Duke knew then that he was the prisoner, not she, because nothing could ever make him leave this sweet, wild woman who arched her back and cried out from the uninhibited pleasure they shared. Seconds later, just as the world fell away from both of them, she grasped his hand tightly and he whispered to her that they were friends as well as lovers.

Afterwards they collapsed, smiling and quiet, on his bed. They rubbed each other with thick bath towels, then snuggled chest to chest. Duke draped one long leg over her, and she nestled a leg between his muscular thighs.

"I feel as if I've loved you forever," she murmured, her mouth brushing his.

"You have. You just didn't know it until two weeks ago."

Shea stroked his angular cheek. "You have poetry in your soul, Alejandro."

"No, sweet, you've got the poetry. I'm going to absorb all your grace and class the way the desert soaks up rain, and maybe, just maybe, I'll get a little civilized."

"Hope not." Shea smiled, but a knot worked in the back of her throat. "I already miss you," she told him in a small distressed tone.

They had, until this moment, avoided discussing the fact that he would be leaving for his ranch in two days. Business demanded that he return; he had a multi-million-dollar racing stable to run. "Come with me," he said firmly.

"For the weekend?"

"Forever."

Shea raised herself on one elbow and studied him with wide eyes. *Forever.* She liked the sound of that word, but not the implications for the estate. "I have to manage Estate Mendocino. The owner is very difficult, but I adore him and don't want to bungle his investment."

"I hereby promote you to executive manager. Now you promote someone to be manager, and let that person handle day-to-day details."

She paled. "Alejandro . . . no . . . don't do this. . . ."

He interrupted her flustered words with a weary nod. "It was just wishful thinking. I know how dear this place is to you. I wouldn't force you to turn it over to another manager. You'd never forgive me, and I couldn't stand that."

Shea joined her mouth to his as completely as their bodies had been joined earlier and poured all her loving appreciation into the kiss.

"Southern California isn't so far from northern California," she whispered when their lips parted. "We'll see a lot of each other. You can count on it." Tears filled her eyes, and she felt a tremor in the smile she gave him. "But it is going to be awfully dull here after you leave."

He raised his finger and smoothed away the dampness on her lower lashes. "You haven't asked me any more about my plans for the estate. Why?"

She gave him a sad, wistful look. "I didn't want to spoil what we've had for the past two days." She hesitated, looking uncomfortable. "And . . . maybe I feel that I don't have a right to question you', since I made the first move the other day . . ."

"In the forest, you mean?" She nodded. "*Querida*, it was inevitable that you and I become lovers. It doesn't matter which of us made the first move."

"Our life together is fated, hmmm?" She caressed his black hair and smiled tenderly at him.

He searched her eyes for a moment, his expression somber. "I'm a betting man, Shea. And I've made a lot of money in a business that depends on intuition and hunches. Could be that I'm a little bit psychic. All I know is that you and I clicked the minute we met. That's never happened to me before."

"Or to me," she assured him.

"Palomino," he murmured, "I'm not going to ruin the estate. Do you want to know what I'm planning? All right—"

"No." She put her hand over his mouth for a second and shook her head. Fear rushed through her, fear that his words were going to ruin this blissful interlude. "Not tonight," she said. "We don't have to talk about it until tomorrow, so let's wait."

They looked at each other for a long moment, and he saw the desperation in her eyes. "All right, *querida*. Roll over on your stomach."

She did as he asked, then Duke adjusted the pillow under her head and spent a minute caressing her damp, golden hair. He propped on one elbow and began to stroke her back soothingly. He let his callused fingers glide over her from neck to rump and back again, his movements slow and steady.

"There, now," he murmured in a cajoling tone. "I have to make you relax, Palomino, so that you'll talk to me. Tell me why this estate is such a sanctuary for you."

He felt her back muscles tense and he bore down on them gently, then rubbed each vertebra of her spine with his thumb. She shivered and let go, sinking deeper into the mattress.

"I like to pretend that the whole world is as peaceful and happy as this estate," she said finally, her voice muffled. "I *like* being sheltered here. I know that's not admirable. I know I'm avoiding the harsher realities of life. But . . . but dammit, I grew up with those realities. I was poor. I was lonely. I was . . ." No she thought suddenly. Now was not the time to tell him just how ugly her childhood had been. Someday, but not now. "I was unhappy," she finished. "Sweetheart, don't blame me for caring so much about the estate. It's my home."

He cupped her shoulder and shook her lightly. "I don't blame you," he said gently, and returned to rubbing her back. "But what do you want from your life, *querida*? Nothing but to spend your spare time exercising your pretty body to even more perfection?" He sighed. "You know, I wouldn't mind if you gained weight."

She laughed softly. "You're kidding, but I love you for it."

"No, really. I can picture you ten years from now, with laugh lines on your face, your body voluptuous . . . I believe, Palomino, that you'll be even more beautiful as you get older."

Words from her childhood echoed in Shea's mind for one tormenting second: *Hell, you'll grow out of it. You're not ugly, even if you are sort of fat. God knows where you got the weight. From your damned father, not from me, that's for sure.*

Shea shut her eyes, and the vivid recollection faded. "Alejandro Araiza," she whispered brokenly, "you're attitude is duly appreciated, but the only time I'll weigh more than I do now is when I'm pregnant."

"That can be arranged."

They were both silent for a moment, absorbing the tingling implications of his remark. "Do you like children?" she asked softly.

"Reckon so. Never been around many. How about you?"

"Reckon so," she mimicked. "Never been around many."

"Maybe we could learn about babies together someday."

Shea turned over and looked up at him with glowing eyes. "Your hints aren't subtle, Alejandro."

His gaze unwavering, he answered very softly, *"Sí."*

She was beginning to realize that he used Spanish to convey his most personal feelings. Pointing at him, she whispered, *"El padre."* Then she pointed to herself. *"La madre."* She smiled tenderly. "I like the way that sounds."

Duke had no more words to express his deep sense of love for her; neither Spanish nor English would do justice to the feeling that he was perfectly whole for the first time in his life. She watched his expression, saw his struggle, then reached up with one graceful hand and touched his lips. She shook her head and smiled in a way that said she understood.

"Sweet dreams, *hombre*."

"Sweet dreams, *querida* Palomino."

Duke turned the lamp off, then lay back and let her pull the sheet and bedspread over them. She slipped into his outstretched arms and put her head on his shoulder. Tomorrow and its problems waited an eternity away.

"Boss, Mr. Araiza is here."

Despite her nervousness, Shea smiled wryly at Jennie's words. "Mr. Araiza" sounded strangely formal, as if it couldn't be the name of the man who'd wakened her this morning by sprinkling bran flakes on her naked chest. A healthy breakfast starts the day off right, he'd explained, and then he'd licked them off her quivering skin, one flake at a time.

"Tell him to come right in, Jennie."

Shea stood, smoothing her hands over her blue jacket and plaid skirt. Her hands trembled, and she swallowed to relieve the tight feeling in her throat. The door opened and Duke walked in. He, too, was dressed for business—tan slacks, a crisp white shirt and dark tie, a light tweed sport coat. A gold tie bar gleamed on his collar, and cuff links made of gold nuggets shown on his shirt cuffs. She inhaled, a little breathless at the change in him. He was devastating but so different.

Then he smiled, and Shea relaxed a little, seeing the reassurance in that smile.

He shut the door lightly, walked over to her desk, and reached across to take her hands in his. "Blues and reds suit you, Ms. Somerton," he said quaintly, eyeing the red blouse she'd coordinated with her outfit. "You create a very impressive business image."

"Your business image is quite impressive, also, Mr. Araiza."

He couldn't resist a personal note. "I wish I'd insisted on walking you home this morning, so that I could watch you dress for work."

"I believe we've started enough rumors for one day. Several people on the staff were out for an early run. They saw me leave your cottage at dawn."

"Did they ask questions?"

"No. They waved, looked embarrassed, and ran faster."

"So? We've got nothing to hide. The rules say staff and guests can't mix. I'm not a guest."

Shea sighed. "When the time's right, I'll make a diplomatic announcement at a staff meeting."

"Just say, 'I have great taste and I've fallen in love with the new owner. And he loves me.' "

"Alejandro, you certainly know how to simplify a situation."

"The name's Mr. Araiza, remember." He gestured toward her desk chair. "Please sit down, Ms. Somerton."

She sat, and he sat down in the guest chair facing her. Shea rubbed the tense muscles in her forehead and eyed him wearily. "This isn't going to work," she said. "I know we agreed to be all business for this meeting, but it feels silly."

His eyes were both somber and sympathetic. "I think it'll be easier this way. Humor me."

Shea nodded. "All right." She exhaled deeply, tried to ignore the thudding of her heart, and placed a note pad in front of her. Shea picked up a pen and poised it over the pad. "Well, Mr. Araiza, now that you've had two weeks to look the estate over, I'd like to know what you think."

His eyes locked on hers and didn't waver. "As a business investment, it's fine. No hassle, management is extremely capable and dependable, and the operation turns a modest but consistent profit. Plus, owning the estate entitles me to a certain amount of social prestige that I didn't have before." He paused. "However, I don't give a tinker's damn about social prestige, and I do care about my conscience. It sticks in my craw to own a place that has no purpose but to pamper a portion of the population that's already too pampered."

Shea nodded again, while dread clutched at her stomach. She knew all this; the important news was still to come. "And therefore, your intentions?" she asked quietly.

"I'm going to divide the estate acreage in half. The half that includes the fat . . . the health spa, will continue under your management."

Shea felt her eyes growing wide with wonder and hope. "Alejandro," she whispered in amazement.

He held up one hand and gave her a warning look. "But I'm going to develop a camp for underprivileged kids on the other half. And those kids will use the estate's facilities on a regular basis."

Shea put her pen down and propped her chin on one fist. She felt stunned. "Which facilities?"

"The pools, the stables. I'll hire a separate staff for the camp—in the state's social services lingo it's called a group home—but I'll also want some of your staff to take part. We'll set up a schedule—specific times when the kids will be on the estate grounds each day. The guests won't be inconvenienced that much."

"What kind of underprivileged kids are we talking about?"

"Like you and I were. Poor. Mostly inner-city kids who've never had a chance to see anything but concrete and smog, and country kids who've never had a taste of anything fancy." He smiled grimly. "When I was growing up I had a lot of, uhmmm, *experience* with organizations that try to help kids like that. Now I'm on the board of directors for several groups. I've already discussed my plans with them, and they're enthusiastic."

"You told me that you knew how to hot-wire a truck by the time you were ten years old," she reminded him, frowning. "Are you hinting that these organizations work with juvenile delinquents?"

"Mild cases. Rowdy kids but basically harmless."

Her throat dry with the turmoil of conflicting emotions, Shea rose and walked to a window. She stood with her back to him, her hands clasped rigidly in front of her. *He's going to resurrect my past,* she thought wretchedly. These kids were living her old life, a painful life she'd struggled to forget.

"Bringing underprivileged teenagers to the estate wouldn't be too risky," she told him, trying to sound calm. "But bringing in juvenile delinquents would invite trouble."

"They'll be supervised."

"There will be problems, regardless. The first time a guest misplaces a piece of jewelry the kids will be suspected, whether they stole it or not."

"We can handle it. I think you're overreacting."

Shea's anger flared. She hurt as if she were being beaten, even though she knew that this plan was noble. She loved him for caring about people, but she couldn't begin to love his plan. Shea whipped around and faced him.

"The estate will lose clients because of this. People pay thousands of dollars a week to stay here. You can't expect them to put up with a bunch of problem teenagers." Duke's expression was slowly darkening, but she rushed on. "Wouldn't it be more feasible to keep the camp separate from the estate? You could build a separate stable, separate pools . . ."

"You love this place. You should understand why I want poor kids to experience it."

"They won't benefit," she countered. "They'll resent it. They'll hurt because they have to leave it to go back to a world that's harsh and disappointing. I know your intentions are good, but what you're proposing is cruel."

Breathing harshly, Shea pivoted and stared out the window again. She heard a soft rustling sound and knew that he had gotten up from the chair. Turning her head, her jaw clenched and shoulders stiff, she watched as he walked over to her. Anger was stamped on his face. He grasped her forearm.

"I think what you really mean is that you don't want a bunch of rough-cut kids to darken the pristine scenery around here," he said in a low voice. "Hell, Shea, is that it? Have I misjudged you so much? I really thought this plan of mine wouldn't upset you."

"I'm not a snob," she told him fiercely. "You *know* that I grew up without much love or help. . . ."

"And you're damned defensive about it. Over the past two days I've told you a lot about myself and the way I grew up. But you refuse to return the favor."

"My life was ugly. I hated it. I made a decision years ago to put it behind me, and I won't dredge it up now."

"Not even to share with me?"

She inhaled raggedly. Tears of frustration and sorrow stung her eyes. "Not even for you, Alejandro."

"Funny kind of love."

"It's the best I can do! It's more love than I've ever given anyone else in my whole life!"

"It's not enough."

She jerked her arm away from him and turned away shivering. "I don't want those kids on the grounds of the estate," she said finally, her voice choked. "I think they'll be unhappy and I think the guests will resent their intrusion. I think there'll be trouble. I like the idea of helping needy kids, but if there was just some other way—"

"No," he interjected curtly. "Why don't you have the guts to tell me how you really feel? Admit it—you're queen bee of an aristocratic little society here, and there's no room for commoners."

Shea hid her anguish behind a glacial stare. "Mr. Araiza, I'll manage the estate however you wish."

"But not happily. I wanted you to feel like a partner, to have the same enthusiasm I have."

"I'm afraid that's not possible. If you want someone else for the job . . ."

"No," he said viciously. "You may be cold, but you're reliable."

She ducked her head, biting her lip to distract the

pain and fury that his words caused. "I am cold, I fear. Cold and heartless and whatever else you're so eager to believe."

"This is tearing me up," he added. "You don't give an inch."

She turned toward him, her eyes flashing. "Do you want a good manager? You've got one. That's enough. You want to force this plan on me regardless of how I feel about it. Don't expect me to be happy."

"The woman I made love to over the past two days is a compassionate person who'd welcome the opportunity to make the world a better place!"

"You don't care about making the world a better place, you just can't bear to let elegance and serenity exist! My world is elegant and serene, and I won't let you ruin it because of the petty malice you developed growing up!"

He grabbed her by the shoulders. "Dammit, don't throw away what we've got because you can't be flexible!"

"You came here and disrupted everything I've worked years to maintain, and now you expect me to adjust without batting an eyelash?"

"I expect you to be the kind of lady I thought you were! I expected you to take these kids to your heart!"

Shea shut her eyes and fought for composure, but the truth bubbled up despite her efforts to ignore it. *I don't want those kids to get close to me. I can't bear their problems, and I don't want to remember mine.* She looked at Duke, measuring the anger and disappointment in his eyes. He'd never understand.

"I'll do whatever you want professionally," she told him in a clipped, formal voice. "But I won't take a personal interest in this project."

A muscle worked in his cheek. "Fine." His voice was lethal and cold. "A construction crew will show up early next week. They'll be working on a site I've already picked out on the other side of the estate. My plan calls for several buildings."

"How long will each group of teenagers stay?"

"Two weeks. With any luck, I'll be able to bring in the first group within a couple of months."

"Fine." They were both distraught; the undercurrent of emotion made shivers run up Shea's spine. "If you'd like," she managed in a tight voice, "you can write the rest of the details and just leave them with Jennie."

"Which translates to 'Get the hell away from me,' " he whispered angrily.

That was too much. Tears slipped down her cheeks. "I love you," she murmured, "but you're hurting me."

He looked down at her with an expression that said he was drowning in regret and anguish. "I don't know what to think," he said. "It never occurred to me that you'd react this damned bad."

"Everything has happened too fast between us. We both need time to figure this out. It's good that you're leaving for your ranch today."

"You think I'm going to leave with this business unsettled between us?"

She stared at him. "How do you want it settled, Alejandro? You want us to pretend that we're not disappointed with each other? I don't think we can."

Breathing roughly, he stepped very close to her and bent his head so that she could hear the low, wounded words he spoke in Spanish. Shea shut her eyes and swayed unsteadily. "I can still feel you and taste you from this morning," he told her. "I can still hear you calling my name. I can remember every word you've spoken to me in the past two days."

Shea nodded. She could recall the same things about him. Vividly. "We were very special together," she said in a barely audible voice.

"*Were,*" he echoed bitterly. "But you don't care."

Without another word, he turned and went to the door. Shea pressed a hand over her mouth to keep from calling out to him as he left the room.

Seven

"Calm down, Red. It's only a dust catcher."

"Pal, that piece of porcelain cost more than my car. If you'd take your hard hat off of it, I'd breathe much easier."

Jennie's words, followed by a squeal of fear and the sound of sudden movement, made Shea hurry out of her office. She found a lanky, blue-jeaned man lounging by a table in the reception area, an orange hard hat grasped lazily in his hands. Jennie stood beside him, clutching the base of a large porcelain vase that wobbled back and forth on the table top. It settled to a stop, and Jennie glared up at the man.

He grimaced. "Sorry," he told Jennie. Then he winked at her and directed his attention to Shea. "Greer O'Malley. Construction contractor," he said politely. "Here to work on the group home. Duke Araiza said that my crew and I could get lunch at the estate every day."

"For safety's sake, we'll serve you on paper plates," Jennie informed him. He was a big, good-looking redhead, and Shea watched with grim amusement as he gave Jennie and her red hair a calm appraisal.

"Bad temper suits you," he quipped. "Makes you look sexy as hell."

Jennie blushed from the collar of her white suit to the top of her head. "You and your men will eat in the kitchen and stay away from the guests," she retorted. "Any more cute remarks and you'll eat in the stables."

"I don't care where we eat, Red, as long as we eat soon. I'm on a tight schedule."

Shea walked over, extended one hand, and introduced herself. She noted that O'Malley's eyes narrowed with intense curiosity when he heard her name. "Mr. Araiza left instructions about you and your men," she told him. "The kitchen has a dining area set up."

"No health food," O'Malley cautioned.

Shea nodded wearily. "As Mr. Araiza instructed, you'll get basic meat-and-potato menus every day."

"Neanderthal food," Jennie interjected airily.

O'Malley growled at her. She retreated behind her desk and sat down with stately disdain. Shea touched the contractor's arm and he returned his attention to her.

"Tell me a little about the work," she asked. "What style are the buildings going to be?"

"They'll look like big log cabins. Duke's in a hurry to get the project finished, so I'm adapting some prefabricated kits to suit his requirements. He wants a two-story main house, a smaller second house, a recreation building, a couple of utility buildings, and a separate cabin for the head counselor. We've just finished grading the primary road, and we'll be hauling materials in by late this afternoon."

"Primary road?" Shea asked in bewilderment.

"A long driveway. It goes to the paved road behind the property. We'll be cutting a second road from the camp to the edge of this property." He gestured around him, indicating the estate.

"A pathway for invading construction workers," Jennie said sardonically. "And later for juvenile delinquents."

O'Malley put one hand on the expensive porcelain vase. "I used to be a delinquent myself. Be nice to me, Red, or I'll have an accident with this doodad."

"You're still a delinquent," Jennie told him.

Shea quickly stepped between them. "We all have work to do," she told them firmly. "Mr. O'Malley, come with me. I'll show you where the kitchen is located, and you can tell me how Alejan . . . Duke is doing. I understand that you're an old friend of his."

"Yeah. See ya, Red."

Jennie eyed him warily. "Not if I see you first."

O'Malley chuckled over that rejoinder as he and Shea walked down a hallway through the main building, but when he stopped laughing Shea became aware of him gazing at her thoughtfully. "So you're a *new* friend of Duke's," he said finally. "Only I doubt *friend* describes the relationship very well." When she looked up at him in surprise, he nodded. "Duke and I are like brothers. He said enough that I could surmise the rest. It's a helluva thing."

"Because he got involved with a coldhearted aristocrat?" she asked wearily. "I suppose that's the way he described me."

O'Malley shook his head. "He hasn't told me much of anything about you. That's how I know that you're very special—Duke has never been closemouthed about his ladies before. When he gave me so few details on the manager of Estate Mendocino—you—I put two and two together. First time I've seen Duke lose his poker face when he talked about a woman. And he's been sleeping outside at night ever since he got back to the ranch."

Shea gasped and stared at O'Malley in bewilderment.

"That was a week ago! What do you mean, sleeping outside?"

O'Malley did a droll Tonto impersonation. "Man put sleeping bag on ground. Get in bag. Sleep. Wake up with dew on face. Ugh."

Exasperated, she ignored his joke. "Why?"

"He sleeps outside when he's got a lot on his mind—been that way ever since we were kids. But I've never heard of him sleeping outside every night for a week before."

"I've been worried about him. We said some painful things to each other, and he was upset when he left the estate."

"He's no worse off than you are, I'd bet. Excuse me for sounding rude, but you look exhausted."

Shea nodded. "I should try sleeping outside," she told him wryly. "It might help."

"Call him. Communicate. I don't know what your disagreement is about, but talking can't hurt."

"We've talked on the telephone," Shea confirmed in a pensive tone. "But we stick to business."

"Stubborn people."

"I'm afraid so. And very different, in ways that are important."

"He's a good man, Shea. But he's tough, and when he wants something, he pushes like hell until he gets it. I watched him take a two-bit ranch and turn it into one of the best Thoroughbred racing stables in the country. He forced the racing community to accept him, and believe me, there were a lot of blue-blooded jackasses who turned their noses up at the grandson of a poor Mexican immigrant."

They stopped by a huge picture window that overlooked one of the back patios. O'Malley whistled softly as he surveyed the guests sitting at the tables there.

"The woman in the red. Is her jogging suit trimmed in mink?"

Shea sighed. "Afraid so."

"Duke said this place was pretentious. I guess he must have fit in about as well as a wolf in a sheep herd."

Shea smiled sadly. "Yes." She paused, gauging her next words, then threw caution to the wind and admitted, "And this sheep fell in love with him."

O'Malley scrutinized her for a moment, then nodded. "Good, because it's just a matter of time before the wolf comes after you."

But he didn't come after her, not the next week or the week after that. Shea forced herself to think about her work and her running, but in the back of her mind she never forgot about Duke. Their phone conversations about his project were maddeningly brusque and formal, and she usually had a headache by the time they ended.

O'Malley kept her updated on the group home's progress, and finally curiosity got the best of her. Late one afternoon she altered her running route and followed the new gravel road that led through the forest at the back of the estate. Ten minutes later she emerged at the small valley that Duke had chosen.

Shea walked slowly around the site, studying the half-finished buildings. She gazed appreciatively at the wooded hills that rose around her and the tiny stream that gurgled down the side of one. Sunset tinted everything with an ethereal pink hue. *Alejandro had chosen a beautiful place.* Her eyes suddenly stinging with tears, she ducked her head and stared at the ground.

She passed the corner of the main house and stepped

up on its low-slung front porch, her head still down in thought, her hands clasped behind her back.

"Shea?"

Shea jumped and jerked her gaze up hurriedly. Duke stood on the porch a few feet away, looking as stunned as she felt. His old jeans and faded safari shirt were stained with dirt and sweat; his face was lined with fatigue. He held a sheaf of blueprints in one big hand.

"Alejandro," she murmured. Shea glanced toward the yard and saw the Ferrari parked among construction machinery and piles of building materials. Hope, excitement, and confusion made her put her hands over her mouth and shut her eyes for a moment. Slowly she opened them and looked back at Duke. "Why didn't you tell me that you were coming here?"

"Didn't know until last night."

Shea absorbed the intense, tormented look in his eyes and began to tremble. He'd been gone for three weeks; it felt like forever. Despite everything that was wrong between them, she was ecstatic at the sight of him. "Are there problems with the construction?"

"No. I just wanted to see how the project was going. I've been working with the crew all day." He gestured toward his dirty clothes. "Sorry," he said sardonically. "My peasant clothes."

Shea's happiness began to fade. "Alejandro," she said in a quiet tone, "you know that I don't care how you're dressed." She pointed at her sweaty blue jogging shorts and matching top, then at the disheveled braid that held her blond hair. "Look at me, for goodness sake."

"I am looking," he muttered. "I can't stop."

Shea inhaled raggedly. "So you drove from one end of the state to the other, on impulse?"

"Lately I've acquired the habit of doing things on impulse."

Shea's expression hardened as anger mixed with her

jumbled emotions. "Romantically, you mean." She stared while he leaned against a porch post, a guarded expression on his face. "When are you leaving again?" she asked.

"Tonight."

"Were you going to see me before you left?"

"Why? Do you have business to discuss?"

Shea was infuriated by his stubborness and frightened by his reserve. She lost all calm and unleashed a torrent in Spanish.

"*Hombre!* How can you stand there and act like ice when you know how much I care about you? You've tortured me for three weeks, and I won't have it anymore! Either fire me or be nice to me, but don't shut me out without a chance!"

He straightened ominously and moved toward her then, frowning, his jaw tight, his back as straight as a redwood tree. When he was close enough to touch her, he spoke in a quiet tone. "I came here because I needed to be near you. I didn't think you wanted to see me, so I wasn't going to visit you or the damned estate."

Shea put her hand on his face. "You think I'm cold and heartless," she whispered brokenly, "but nothing has ever hurt me so much as when you walked out of my office three weeks ago."

"Don't touch me," he warned softly. "It isn't smart right now."

"I don't want to be smart." Shea slid both arms around his neck and pressed her body to his. Before he could move back, she kissed him.

He twisted his lips away and grasped her arms, his fingers digging in sharply. "Stop."

"You think that I'm too elegant and calm to seduce you, Alejandro? You're wrong. I can be just as lusty and demanding as you."

She curled her body against his torso and angled her

head to kiss him again. The unfettered wildness was a foreign and overwhelming sensation that drained her of reservations. "Regardless of everything," she said against his mouth, "we belong together. You used to say the same thing. What happens with the estate or this camp doesn't matter. Alejandro, you're back, and that's all I care about."

He gave a hoarse moan and grabbed her in a fierce embrace, then submitted to her sweet torment and returned the kiss, his mouth rough and greedy. One hand slid down her spine and over her rump, pulling her up on her toes, pulling her forward so that their lower bodies meshed intimately.

Shea buried her head against his shoulder and hugged him with all her strength. He kissed her hair, then dipped his head and whispered hoarsely against her ear.

"I want you so bad that I could strip off your clothes and make love to you right here on the porch. I've never missed anyone as much as I've missed you. I've never needed anyone as much as I need you." He paused, breathing so hard that she slid one hand down and stroked his chest anxiously. "But I have to leave, *querida*."

Shea lifted her head and gazed at him speechlessly. His dark eyes were filled with regret but also determination as they burned into her. "If we make love right now, it'll only complicate the problem. Nothing would be solved and we'd hurt each other more."

"I love you, Alejandro."

His voice was troubled but gentle. "Enough to forget your doubts about this project of mine? Enough to forget that you resent what I'm trying to do? Can you do more than pretend to be enthusiastic?"

Shea leaned her forehead against his shoulder and said sadly. "You ask for so much."

"You have so much to give."

"I'm trying."

"So am I, Palomino. I want to prove to you that our worlds aren't so different."

"Bringing underprivileged kids to the estate will do that?"

He stroked her hair. "I hope so."

Shea quivered and gently pushed herself away from him. He looked down at her with concern and sorrow. *"Hombre,"* she said in a voice that strained for lightness, "you're a tough horse to tame."

He managed a chuckle, though it was a pained sound. "I'll never be tame, and I hope you won't be either."

"Do you have to leave right away?"

Duke nodded. "I have to be back at the ranch by tomorrow morning. And if I stay with you much longer, I'll . . . never mind."

"I'd never turn you loose. You're right. Go."

"Come on, I'll give you a ride to the estate."

Shea shook her head. She couldn't keep up this nonchalant facade that long. "I'll run back the way I came. If I hurry, I'll be home before dark."

"You'll ride in my car," he said firmly. "I don't like the idea of you running through the forest when it's getting dark."

"Alejandro, I may be a sheep, but I can take care of myself."

He frowned in bewilderment. "A sheep? What the hell?"

"Nothing. It has to do with something O'Malley said."

"You two are trading strange philosophies?"

"O'Malley is chasing Jennie Cadishio. I'm their referee. I talk to him almost every day." She turned and stepped off the porch, aching from the strain of continuing their gentle banter. Duke walked with her to the edge of the clearing, where the new road led back to the estate. Shea stopped and looked up at him. "I can barely force myself to leave you." She reached for him, but he shook his head.

His expression was almost harsh from the effort of restraining himself. "If we kiss good-bye, you'll be in a helluva lot of trouble. I'd forget all my noble intentions. I'd put you in the Ferrari and take you to the ranch with me, and then I'd use every tactic short of force to keep you there. Away from the damned fat farm we'd have a better chance of being happy."

"The damned fat farm," she echoed, frowning sadly. She let her hands drop back by her sides. "You hate it so much. Oh, Alejandro."

"I'm trying not to," he said in a hoarse tone.

She gave him a bittersweet smile and knew that she had to leave right away or she'd cry. "Good-bye," she murmured, the words barely audible.

He took her hands, lifted them, and kissed her palms. For a moment he pressed his face there, his eyes closed. *"Good night,"* he told her. "Never good-bye."

The morning breeze swept across the desert panorama, then crept up the rocky slopes to the ridge where Duke sat on a huge palomino stallion. The breeze whispered over Duke's face, bringing the arid, clean smell of the desert with it. The stallion snorted at the invigorating fragrance and shifted impatiently. The wind made a rustling sound in the low chaparral shrubs that were so typical of this part of southern California. Overhead a teal blue sky was emerging from the cover of night.

"Someday, Outlaw," Duke told the horse softly, "we'll bring Shea here to see the desert wake up." He either spoke those words or thought them every morning when he came to this spot. The ritual had begun after he left her at the estate the first time; now that he had left her there again, the ritual was even more important.

"Maybe I'm a fool for leaving her, eh?" Duke murmured. The stallion snorted again. "It's been two days, and it seems like two years. She *wanted* me to stay. If I didn't love her so much, that would have been easy to do." The stallion pawed the ground fiercely. "Patience," Duke whispered, as much to himself as to Outlaw.

With one nudge of the reins Duke swung the big stallion around and guided him toward the distant, green oasis that marked the Solo Verde ranch. Thirty minutes later the crisp white fences of the outlying pastures bordered Outlaw on both sides, and in five minutes more Duke reined the stallion to a halt by the first of several large barns.

"Señor Duke!" A wizened little man with bow legs and silver-white hair hurried out of the barn and grasped Outlaw's bridle. He looked up at Duke worriedly.

"Luís, I'm going to put you on the track one day and clock you," Duke joked lightly. "I bet you do a helluva quarter mile. What's wrong?"

"You have a visitor at the house!"

Duke glanced at the sun rising in a golden explosion to the east, then swung down off Outlaw's back and handed Luís the reins. "At this hour? Who?"

"A very pretty lady!"

"Hmmm. What's her name?"

"Shea Somerton."

Duke broke into a run.

She was seated in his large den on a rugged *equipal* made of tanned pigskin and rough-hewn wood, looking as out of place as an orchid in a cactus patch. She was dressed in a flowing blue dress with a dark print scarf arranged artfully around her shoulders. Her hair was swept up in a mass of blond curls. But despite her flawless appearance, she looked haggard around the eyes, and makeup couldn't hide the redness there. Duke knelt down in front of her and grasped both her hands. She looked at him calmly.

"What's happened?" he asked. "What's wrong?"

Her eyes were pensive. "Nothing, really. I'm resigning as manager of the estate."

"*What?*"

"I wanted to tell you in person. I wanted to tell you right away, so that I couldn't change my mind. I flew to San Diego last night and rented a car to drive here."

Speechless, Duke simply stared at her for a moment. He shook his head as if to clear it. "You're *resigning*? What the hell . . ."

"I can't fight you, and I can't fight what I feel about your project."

"I don't want you to leave the estate."

She gave him a look of determination. "It's the only way. I won't have any trouble finding a new job; my qualifications are excellent. And maybe with the issue of the estate out of the way, you and I—"

"You're the heart of the estate, dammit." He stood, feeling angry and bewildered. "I won't accept your resignation."

She stood also, her hands clasped in front of her over a tiny blue purse. "I'm doing this for *us*, Alejandro," she explained firmly. "I've waited all my life for you, and I won't let this problem drive you away again."

"You love me that much?" he asked hoarsely.

Her voice trembled and her violet eyes narrowed as she fought tears. "Of course I do, *hombre*. This is my way of giving you everything you want. Love. Enthusiasm. If I participate in your group-home project from a distance, I think I can enjoy it."

He jerked the purse out of her hands and tossed it onto a chair, then pulled her into his arms. "Not like this, *querida*," he insisted, his voice becoming gentle. "I don't want you to give up everything you've worked for."

"I'm resigning, Alejandro. That's firm."

He frowned. "Hell, no, you hard-headed woman."

Her eyed widened with annoyance. "Look, don't try to bully me."

He glared down at her and searched his mind for a solution to this dilemma. She couldn't quit, even if her reason made him adore her more than ever. "The estate won't be anything but a hassle to me if you're not there to run it," he told her. "If you quit, I'll close it down."

"That's not fair!" She pushed him away and stepped back, breathing hard.

Duke nodded to her with grim resignation. "I only play fair in poker and business," he warned. "This is personal. I'm going to get what I want, and what I want is for you to keep running the fat farm."

"You wouldn't shut it down. You wouldn't put everyone on the staff out of work. You're bluffing, poker man."

"Maybe, maybe not. That's a risk you don't want to take," he told her.

"And you accuse me of being cold and heartless!"

Duke put a hand over the left side of his chest. "Nothing here but ice," he said drolly.

"Alejandro, I'm resigning for the sake of our relationship!"

"You're not resigning. I love you too much to let you give up the fat—the estate. I'll learn to like the place, if that'll make you feel better."

"Look, I really think I know best . . ."

"You're worn out and upset. How can you know best? Enough said."

He grabbed her suddenly and picked her up. She

yelped in a most unsophisticated way and wriggled angrily, then lambasted him in loud Spanish when he refused to put her down. He stood unmoving, gazing at her sternly until she finished.

"I've never been compared to so many different animals before," he admitted. "And most of them ugly." He started down a corridor in the big, Spanish-style ranch house, carrying her easily.

"Put me down, Alejandro," she said between clenched teeth.

"I'll put you down in my bed. You'll get some sleep, and then you'll go back to Mendocino. I can't have my manager running around southern California when she's got work to do."

"Damn your time!"

He walked into a large and very masculine room that resembled the lair of an old-West bandit who'd acquired plenty of gold. Rough-hewn timbers lined the ceiling; Indian blankets decorated the white-washed walls; the floor consisted of big, unpolished clay tiles strewn with colorful rugs, and the heavy Southwestern-style furniture looked as if it had been designed for Paul Bunyan.

Duke dumped her onto the jumbled sheets and blankets of his king-size bed. "Can I get you anything before you go to sleep?" he asked politely.

With her legs splayed and a ringlet of hair hanging over her eyes, Shea felt less than dignified. She propped herself on both elbows and glared up at him. "I couldn't get you to make love to me the other evening and I can't get you to let me resign," she fumed. "Just exactly what do you intend to do with me?"

"I'll let you know my long-range plans later. For right now, I intend to turn you into a den mother for a bunch of kids who desperately need all your gentleness and patience."

"I don't feel gentle or patient!"

"That's because you're sleepy."

"I'm not sleepy!"

He sat down beside her, put one brawny hand on her shoulder, and blithely shoved her flat on the bed. "You will be," he promised. Shea rolled away from him and sat up. She grasped her forehead quickly and went still.

"You make me dizzy," she muttered.

"You're exhausted." Duke reached over and put one hand on her back, stroking softly. She trembled, and the tightness in her shoulders eased a little.

"I dread meeting the kids from your group home," she told him abruptly. "They're going to remind me of everything I left behind."

"Lay down." He guided her back until she lay with her head pillowed on his thigh. She looked up at him sadly, and he caressed her face with his fingertips. "I know you had an ugly childhood," he began.

"You don't know how ugly, Alejandro."

"Sssh. When you're ready to tell me, I'll listen. But you can't run from it forever, *querida*."

They became silent, and time passed without notice as she lost herself in his loving eyes. All the energy and resistance drained out of her. Shea blinked languidly as his fingers trailed back and forth across her forehead. "If I seem coldhearted toward your project," she said, and now her voice was low and sleepy, "it really does have to do with the way I grew up."

"Sssh, *querida*, I'm beginning to understand that."

"I'm no . . . snob."

"I know, I know. Sssh. I'm sorry I ever accused you of that."

"I'll . . . try to cooperate . . . with . . . enthusiasm." Gathering one last ounce of rebellion, she squinted at him. "Bully," she said without much malice. "I wanted to resign."

"No, you wanted to make things better between us. Things are fine with us, Palomino." He brushed his fingers across her lips. His voice dropped. "Sleep now. I love you."

"Hmmm. I love you."

Her eyes closed and remained shut. He slid his arms under her, moved her so that her head rested on a pillow, then took her hair down and spread its lustrous strands around her face. "A halo," he whispered.

"Hmmm. Flattery."

Duke was filled with such tenderness for her that he couldn't say anything else. Her breathing slowed and he knew that she slept. Working carefully, he undressed her. After he arranged the covers over Shea's relaxed, naked body, he rose and went to the wide, glass-paned doors that opened onto a private courtyard at the center of his home. Sunlight filtered over him while he lazed, smiling, against a door jamb and watched Shea sleep. At least for the moment, everything in the world was golden.

Eight

If the population of Beverly Hills ever rioted, this is what it would look like, Shea decided as she gazed around her crowded office. It was as though Gucci, Givenchy, Yves St. Laurent, and Adolfo had organized a sit-in.

She held up both hands and spoke calmly to the worried guests who'd just received notice of Duke's project. "These kids will be supervised every minute they're on the estate grounds. They won't affect the schedule of classes or your use of the facilities. They'll spend most of their time at their own place, which will remain entirely separate from the estate."

"But they're . . . they're *criminals*," protested a woman who wore a pink tennis dress to match her hair.

"I could go to L.A. and jog the streets if I wanted punks to watch me exercise," someone else commented.

"There's nothing to be concerned about," Shea assured everyone. "These kids aren't candidates for San Quentin; they're good kids who just need a little guidance."

"Boys. All boys," a lithe, fidgety male guest noted

sarcastically. "If I wish to see juvenile delinquents, I'll go visit my sons."

"The boys will only be here for two weeks," Shea explained to him. "The group after that is all girls. The plan is to alternate."

"Great. Teenage hoodlum girls. I did the sound track for a movie about their type. It was called *Lips And Chains*."

Shea's cajoling mood began to fade. Duke was right about some of the estate's guests—they *were* obnoxiously self-centered and pampered. She struggled for tactful words, but a gravelly female voice interrupted her.

"What are ya?" the voice demanded of everyone. "A bunch of snobs?"

Shea watched in amazement as a small, robust woman elbowed her way out of the crowd and gazed lethally at her fellow guests. Sally Rogers, four-time Emmy winner, two-time Oscar nominee, was a legend among comic actresses. She wore a flowing caftan and so much bulky jewelry that she looked like a human Christmas tree. Her long, artfully tangled auburn hair had long since forgotten its natural color.

"What's your beef?" Sally asked, eyeing the crowd. "Afraid some teenage slob is gonna spit in the pool? Come on, people. Nobody's gonna bother us. Hell, maybe we need to be bothered. By the way, I grew up in a tough part of New Jersey. You guys ought to worry about my habits, not about a bunch of wet-nosed kids."

Shea silently vowed to add every one of Sally's movies to her tape collection. "Thank you, Ms. Rogers." To the other guests, she added, "That's right. None of these teenagers will bother you. You have my word on it."

As the guests filed out, looking uncertain and unhappy, Sally Rogers gave Shea a thumbs-up. Shea smiled wanly and sat down at her desk. One ally out of 123 guests, she thought. Not good bettin' odds, as Alejandro would say.

Alejandro. She studied her calendar wistfully. He'd promised to come back to the estate as soon as he could, but he had to organize the ranch's business first. That way he'd be able to stay indefinitely when he returned.

"Boss. Ohh, boss." Jennie stepped into the office, shut the door behind her, and smiled apologetically. "Another group of guests are here to ask you about Duke's camp for wayward children."

Shea grasped her throat dramatically. "Lions and tigers and bears. Oh, my."

"That's right, Dorothy, we're not in Kansas anymore," Jennie noted. She opened the office door wide and began motioning people inside.

"Your Highness, I assure you that you have no need of bodyguards under the new circumstances," Shea murmured into the phone. "These aren't . . . no . . . we're not starting a terrorist training camp next door. Yes. Basic American kids. Like Michael J. Fox on *Family Ties*? No, not quite like that, but you have nothing to worry about. Yes. *Shok-no ben armen* to you, as well. And please convey my greetings to your wives."

Shea hung up and stared wearily out the back window of her cottage. It was nearly midnight, which meant that it was daytime in the South China Sea. Prince Shalukan had called as soon as he received her letter about the estate's new focus.

Bone tired and depressed, she pulled her robe tighter around her, padded to the kitchen, and poured herself a glass of wine. "Here's to trouble," she muttered, and downed it in three big swallows. Coughing, Shea went to the living room and lay on the couch. Within thirty seconds she fell asleep.

Sometime later she had a highly sensual dream in which Alejandro nibbled her neck and ran his hands under her robe. Suddenly Shea realized that she wasn't dreaming. She opened her eyes to find the man of her dreams grinning at her.

"Hombre!" she exclaimed.

"Surprise, surprise, surprise." His grin was replaced by a hungry half smile that made her heart rate leap. "Lord, woman, I've missed you the past week."

"You're here early!"

"I got business settled sooner than I expected. So I hopped into the Ferrari and hit the trail for Mendocino. Did I upset your schedule?"

Shea blinked the remnants of sleep from her eyes and shook her head fervently. Happiness filled her with giddy excitement. "No!" She threw both arms around his neck and pulled him to her for a kiss that was both wanton and tender.

Laughing, he lay down on top of her, and she wrapped her legs around his blue-jeaned hips. Shea stripped his white windbreaker off his shoulders. He wore a faded work shirt underneath, and the contrast between the soft material and his hard torso was irresistible. Shea sighed as she ran her hands down his long, muscled back and pulled his hips closer.

"Welcome back," she whispered in Spanish.

"A wild mare. Hmmm. *Bueno.*" Duke kissed her face and neck while his arms slid under her in a tight, possessive embrace. "I wanted to do this at the ranch. Did you have any idea what it did to me to watch you sleep naked without touching you?"

"I had a plane to catch. You forced me to leave as soon as I woke up!"

"For your own good. I was on the verge of holding you hostage in my bedroom."

"*Bandolero*," she called him in a gentle tone.

He studied her eyes for a moment, then frowned. "You look tired, *querida*. And a little pale."

"I spent the whole day putting out fires."

"Ah. You notified the clientele that the *loco* owner is making some changes in the estate. And?"

"People are worried. But we have a couple of allies, at least." She told him about Sally Rogers.

"What a lady," he said with respect.

"And Chip Greeson called from Burbank. He said you've blown your chance to get the estate featured on *Lifestyles of the Rich and Famous*. And that he's going to create a new game show in your honor. *Dialing for Delinquents*. He also said that he admires you tremendously."

Duke looked at her with great tenderness. "You've done a helluva job setting this up, Palomino. I know it still isn't easy for you to get behind the project."

She nodded. "I'm keeping an open mind."

"And I love you for it."

"I love you. . . . What are you doing?"

He pushed himself up and sat on the couch, then pulled her upright too. Her legs were still draped around him, and he ran a hand up one thigh. His eyes half shut, he smiled in a greedy, impatient way that was very masculine and very erotic.

"You're naked under this robe," he noted. "I'm taking you to bed."

"Ah. I thought you'd never ask."

After they were both naked and under the covers, he held her spoon-style. As he stroked her breasts, his arousal pressed against the backs of her thighs. She moved seductively, encouraging it.

"My poor, tired *querida*," he murmured into her ear. "I feel the tension in you. You're quivering."

"I'm tried, but I'm trembling because I want you so much, Alejandro."

He groaned softly. "Relax, love, and I'll take care of you."

Duke pulled the covers away from their bodies and Shea turned to lay on her back. Passion gathered inside her like a wild storm as he began to nuzzle and lick the taut peaks of her breasts.

Shea's head tilted back on the pillow and she shut her eyes. She and Alejandro were floating in the middle of the night, just the two of them, lost in a world that was only sensation and sound. She heard the sweet, soft sucking noises his mouth made on her body as he moved his attention downward. She felt his hands parting her legs. Teasing her, then carefully learning her intimacies as if he were loving her for the first time.

His mouth followed, and he tantalized her. Shea wound her fingers into his hair as he cherished the most tender skin. He was rough, then gentle, mixing the contrasts skillfully so that she never knew what to expect. His hands held her hips and raised her body so that he could please her even more. He groaned against her, his breath hot. Shea sensed his desperate restraint and realized that he was trembling violently.

"Come here," she begged. "I can wait."

Duke raised his head for just a moment and kissed her inner thigh. "Sssh. I have so much to give. Take it. Take it and know how much your pleasure means to me."

Shea had never received such a loving, unselfish gift. Calling his name with husky cries she let the caress of his mouth and tongue drive her beyond rational thought. When her body's sweet turbulence finally quieted, she was crying.

"No, no," Duke murmured anxiously, and moved upwards to take her head between his hands. He wondered if he'd upset her in some way. "What's wrong, *querida*?"

Her violet eyes were luminous behind the sheen of tears, and she smiled. "I'm really certain now, Alejandro. I *know* how it feels to be loved. And I know how much I love you, because . . . a moment ago, I realized that I'd die for you."

Whispering her name, Duke sheathed himself in her welcoming body. He smiled back at her, his chest nearly bursting with emotion, and she reached a hand up to gently brush away the tears he gave her in return.

The first group of teenagers arrived at the Mendocino Group Home on a hot July afternoon. Duke had hired a husband-wife team of social workers to manage the home, and they hired two assistants who had previous experience with group-home programs.

As Duke watched a dozen boys drag their meager luggage off the home's new van, he kept telling himself that Shea's worries were unfounded. These teens and the groups that followed in the weeks to come would benefit from contact with the estate. There wouldn't be any trouble.

One of the counselors walked up and handed Duke a list of names. "This is what we have. A colorful group." The counselor paused, and grinned. "I've worked with worse."

"Don't scare me, son," Duke told him wryly. He scanned the list, looking at the notes beside each boy's name. "Petty theft, fighting at school, disobeys parents, seduced several teachers at his high school . . ." Duke blinked and looked at the last entry again. "Parker Jones, sixteen, seduced several teachers?"

"Afraid so, Duke."

"Hell, I was bad, but I never went after teachers." Feeling grimly amused Duke glanced at the boy. "Which one is the lover?"

"Tall kid with the brown hair and the muscles."

The kid was good looking and walked with a confident swagger. Duke watched him carry an old duffel bag into the house. With a sigh Duke tossed the name chart back to the counselor. "Whatever you do, keep that underage stud away from the estate's female guests."

"Got it." The counselor walked away, nodding his head.

Trouble, Duke thought in dismay. He could smell it in the hot wind, and he wanted to avoid it at all costs. Shea was trying so hard to accept his project, and he was trying to make her happy in return. He'd let her teach him how to meditate. She'd weaned him off coffee and gently gotten him to trade his three-egg breakfasts for oatmeal or cold cereal. He'd never felt better—or more worried about the future.

Shea came back from her evening run to find Duke stretched out on her couch, asleep, wearing nothing but a pair of gym shorts. A crumpled beer can lay on his flat stomach. She tiptoed to him and whisked the can away carefully, noting as she did that he seemed to be frowning in his sleep.

Several days had passed since the boys' arrival at the group home. She'd avoided meeting the teenagers, and Duke hadn't pressured her. She loved him for that. She also loved him for taking a hotel room in Mendocino so that the staff wouldn't gossip about his presence at her cottage. The staff knew about their relationship, she felt certain; the lack of questions so far was evidence of everyone's devotion to her and their fondness for Duke.

Shea went to the bathroom, removed her sweaty jogging outfit, and put on her robe. She ran cool water over a washcloth and carried it back to the couch. Kneeling beside Duke, she wiped his forehead. My *hombre* is exhausted, she thought anxiously. His dark eyes opened slowly, and he gave her a groggy smile.

"Long day?" she whispered.

He nodded slightly. "Good day, though. Jason only called me a son of a bitch once today, and I only threatened to kick his butt once. I think we're making progress."

Shea sighed, then leaned over and kissed his nose in sympathy. Jason Greggers was one of the tougher kids, and he was only thirteen years old. "You need to leave the counseling to the counselors," she said.

"I know. My Lord, after this, breaking colts will be a breeze. I played basketball with twelve energetic teenagers for three hours nonstop. I feel real old right now."

"Alejandro, you're in your prime. You're just worn out from lack of sleep." She arched one brow at him. "You have nighttime *responsibilities* that those teenagers can't begin to fathom."

Duke thought about Parker Jones, the high-school Romeo, and his mouth crooked up in a tight smile.

"I think I'll drive you over to the hotel soon and put you to bed early," she informed him.

"Only if you'll spend the night with me. I don't want to ignore my responsibilities."

She sighed theatrically. "Oh, I *suppose* no one would notice if I didn't come back to the estate until tomorrow morning." She paused, and her humor faded into concern. "Alejandro, are you worried about something?"

Duke took evasive action. "Hmmm. Why?"

"You were frowning in your sleep a minute ago."

"I must have been dreaming about you."

"Well, what a compliment," she said in dismay.

"Yeah . . . now I remember . . . you were trying to seduce me in a mud bath, and you kept saying, 'This little piggy went to market, this little piggy went home, and *this* little piggy . . .' That's when it got real disgusting . . ."

"Oh, hush!" Laughing, she began to whack him with the washcloth.

The next afternoon Shea stopped by the reception area for the massage and mud-bath rooms. As she bent over an appointment book, noting a schedule change, a female guest came bouncing out of the dressing room. The woman was a fortyish business executive with a slender, well-kept body clothed in colorful print shorts and a barely buttoned white shirt. She was barefoot, and her face was brightly flushed. When she spotted Shea, she laughed merrily and grabbed her hand.

"The new masseur is extraordinary, darling."

Before Shea could reply, the woman breezed out of the area. Shea was humming the theme song from *The Summer of '42*. She frowned, bewildered. *What* new masseur? She had to approve all staff hirings, and there was no new massage therapist.

"Hi, there. Are you next?"

Shea studied the tall young man who stepped into the reception area. His brown hair was a little ruffled, and *his* face was flushed. He wore baggy white shorts and a blue T-shirt with the slogan Once Is Never Enough. The slow head-to-toe look he gave her was followed by a jaunty smile.

"You sure do justice to that sundress," he told her. "White's a terrific color on you."

Shea clasped her hands in front of her and struggled to imitate Duke's best poker face. "Why, thank you," she answered calmly. "I don't believe we've met before."

"My name's Parker."

"My name's Shea. Shea Somerton. I'm the manager here, and I don't recall hiring you."

The blood drained out of his face. "Oh, damn." He groaned. "Are you Araiza's chick?"

Shea nodded grimly and gave him a puzzled look. "Who are you?"

"Uh, never mind. I was just . . . it was a joke . . . I gotta go . . ."

"Freeze, mister," she said sternly. "I want to see a guest card or your visitor's pass."

He grimaced, stared at her open mouthed, then plopped down in a chair and tossed his hands in a gesture of defeat. "I'm from the group home," he admitted. "We came over to swim and I sort of went exploring."

Shea stared at him, stunned. "Did you just finish giving a massage to one of the female guests?" she asked between clenched teeth.

Parker grasped his chest dramatically. "I just . . . I swear I just came in here to see what it was all about, and this lady walked in, and she thought I was a massage guy, so she got undressed and—"

"Forget the details," Shea interjected. "How old are you?"

"Sixteen."

Oh, Lord. She searched her mind for any information on California's laws concerning minor males and adult females. Not that Parker looked like he'd been victimized.

Shea pointed toward the door. "Out. Go back to the pool and—"

"*There* you are." A counselor out of breath and obviously upset, burst into the room. He glanced at Shea, his face red with apology. "I won't blame you if you raise hell, Ms. Somerton. Romeo—I mean Parker—was my responsibility, and I let him get out of sight. I'll tell Duke what happened."

Shea was seething, but she realized that both she and the counselor were in a predicament. He didn't want to suffer Duke's wrath, and she didn't want to draw attention to the fact that the estate was now providing sex therapy along with massages. She looked from the counselor to Parker.

"Fellows, this is our secret." She pointed at Parker. "But I'll wring your neck if I catch you 'wandering' again."

"You're an okay lady," Parker noted, looking relieved.

"Thanks, Ms. Somerton," the counselor added.

Another female guest hurried into the reception area at that moment. She looked impatient and excited. "I came to make an appointment with the new masseur," she announced, "Parker."

"*Querida*, you seem distracted tonight."

They were seated in rocking chairs on the balcony outside Duke's hotel room. The hotel was one of Mendocino's Victorian relics, a marvelous old building that fronted main street. Beyond the street stretched a field of tall grass. The field ended at steep slopes that plunged to the Pacific. Shea stared at a panorama of moonlit ocean and tried to keep her anger from surfacing.

"I'm just tired," she told him.

"You hardly spoke during dinner."

"I ran several extra miles after work. My legs hurt."

He turned his chair to face her, then patted one knee. "Put those hooves up here, filly, and let old Duke rub your fetlocks."

"No, thanks. I've got to go back to the estate. I have some paperwork to do." Shea continued staring at the ocean, but she sensed his annoyance and puzzlement in the silence that followed her remark.

"Palomino," he said in a soft, warning tone, "something's wrong and you've got to tell me what it is."

"Nothing's wrong."

"Let's see. The boys came over today and went swimming. If I hadn't had to stay here and take some phone calls, I would have come with them. I told you that earlier. Did they say anything wrong or disturb any of the guests? Did the counselors keep things under control?"

Disturb wasn't an adequate description for what Parker had done to a guest, Shea thought glumly. "I don't like having them around," she said in a sharp voice. "They worry me more than I ever thought they would. They're loud and rowdy."

"Most teenagers are. They were only there for an hour, weren't they? And didn't you assign them one of the indoor pools away from the guests?"

"Yes. Yes." Her back muscles felt as if they'd snap from the tension of keeping Parker's escapade to herself. She couldn't bear to get the counselor in trouble with Duke. She also felt sorry for Parker himself, who would probably be sent back to his Los Angeles home immediately if she reported his indiscretion.

The counselor had explained to her in private that Parker lived with a boozing older sister and her abusive husband. Shea remembered her own childhood, and her animosity toward Parker had evaporated.

"Shea?" Duke's voice was serious. "What happened to your cooperative attitude and open mind?"

"This new situation is putting me under a lot of strain," she answered. "You can't expect me to adjust easily." She was glad that the dim light hid her confusion and sadness. "*Adíos.* I'll see you tomorrow."

As Shea walked inside the hotel she heard Duke cursing no one and everyone.

He let her strange mood simmer until the next night, and then he showed up at her cottage bearing a bottle of tequila and a box filled with Mexican food.

"There's only one way to end a fight," Duke informed her as he strode into the kitchen. "And that's by sharing good liquor and hot food."

"I know your idea of hot food. Let me get a fire extinguisher."

He didn't laugh at the joke or acknowledge her wistful glances and outstretched hands. With single-minded reserve he went about the business of getting two plates from her kitchen cabinet, then dished up an array of Mexican concoctions.

"I was bad tempered last night," she admitted. "I don't expect you to understand."

"Doesn't matter. I love you anyway." He walked past her into the dining room, his expression set in a mask of determination. "That's what love's about. Putting up with each other's bad moods."

"Sounds romantic," she said sardonically.

"Doesn't always have to be romantic. Just permanent and loyal." He breezed past her again and got a shot glass for his tequila. "Want some booze?"

"No. I'll drink water."

"So be it." He filled a glass for her, then brusquely grabbed napkins and silverware from the kitchen drawers.

"Alejandro Araiza, stop playing kitchen maid and look at me!" she ordered, exasperated. "I feel as if I'm a chore you have to attend to!"

He gazed calmly at her. "Don't look a gift horse in the mouth. I intended to wait until you came to me. But nooo, the elegant and proud Ms. Somerton won't apologize. . . ."

"I apologize," she murmured. Then, more fervently, "I *apologize*, Alejandro." She stomped over to him and hugged his neck. "I was an ornery beast last night, and I needed to be by myself. A minute ago I was getting ready to drive over to the hotel and beg your forgiveness."

He hesitated briefly, then hugged her neck. "You've got to talk to me about what upsets you," he said firmly.

"I was going to bring you a dinner of tofu salad and herbal tea. . . ."

"Lord, I'm glad I decided to make the first move."

They were interrupted by the sound of running feet and rustling shrubs outside the cottage. "What now?" Shea exclaimed as Duke rushed to the door. "Don't! I'll call security!"

But he was already outside. Shea ran after him. The sounds came from behind the cottage. Duke and Shea rounded the corner in time to see Sally Rogers, dressed in a silky red caftan, make an amazingly accurate flying tackle on someone much smaller. Both Sally and the intruder went down in the shrubbery.

"Cool it, kid. Cool it!" the famed comedienne squawked.

"Ouch! You're twisting my ear!"

"I'll twist it off and bronze it for you if you don't get still!"

"All right, all right! I wasn't doin' nothing!"

"You were looking in my cottage window, you little creep!"

"So what? So sue me, you fat broad."

"Fat broad? You weasel." She was now sitting on the intruder, and he was wheezing for breath. Sally began to laugh. "I haven't had this much fun in years!"

Shea followed Duke through the shrubs and stopped, speechless with disbelief, as he knelt down beside Sally. He bent over and eyed the person under her. "Jason, what are you doing away from the group home?"

"She's squashing me, Duke! Damn . . ."

"Don't cuss, weasel," Sally ordered.

"Okay, okay! I was just restless, man. I just took a long walk, you know, and I looked in a window, and then this lady comes screeching out and almost kills me!"

"I might yet," Sally told him.

Shea stepped forward. "I hope you're not hurt," she told Sally. "I can't begin to apologize enough—"

"No problem! It was fun! I haven't had anybody peek in my windows in so long I decided that I couldn't let this brave turkey get away! Had to capture his little fanny and see who he was."

Duke sat back on his heels. "I'll say one thing for you, Sal, your aerobics class is paying off."

Laughing again, Sally got off of Jason and settled beside him in a heap of red caftan. Duke took the small, spindly boy by the shirt collar and helped him sit up. Shea took a long look at the thin black face made memorable by enormous brown eyes that snapped with intelligence. So this was Jason, the little warrior who'd had the courage to call Alejandro impolite names. He looked very young and very alone.

At that sight, Shea was a goner. She had been this kind of defensive little person once, and she'd often felt just the way Jason looked. She held out a hand.

"C'mon, Peeping Jason. How about some Mexican food?"

He looked at her askance. "Who are you?" he demanded.

"Possibly the only friend you've got right now."

"I catch your drift." He took her hand and wobbled to his feet.

Shea glanced at Sally. "Would you like some Mexican food and tequila?"

She grinned. "Now that's what I came to this fat farm for. Sure."

As the four of them sat around the dining room table and ate, Shea continued to feel Duke's scrutiny. She was tired and upset at the incidents involving the teenagers, but she couldn't turn away from Jason. Her emotions in turmoil, she picked at her food and said very little.

Jason and Sally struck up a strange, bantering friendship that resulted in an even stranger happening: Jason apologized for calling her a fat broad. After that Sally looked at him with growing adoration, and Duke gave in easily when she insisted on walking Jason to the group home.

She and Jason ambled off in the darkness, swinging flashlights and telling each other bad jokes. Duke called the head counselor, explained the situation, and directed him to give Sally a ride back to her cottage. When he got off the phone, he came to the kitchen and pried Shea away from the dishwasher.

"You're fantastic," he told her in a husky tone. "You surprised yourself, didn't you? You thought you could resist the kids."

"Can't I be mysterious?" she retorted sharply. "You told me once that you like mystery in a woman."

Suddenly, now that they were alone, she couldn't hold her emotions in check any longer. Tears slipped down her cheeks.

"Shea?" Duke said anxiously.

"Let's go to bed," she whispered in a broken voice. "I just want to be quiet and feel your arms around me."

"But what's wrong?"

"I don't want to talk. Please." She put a finger over his mouth and shook her head. "Please."

His eyes were troubled, but he nodded and drew her to him for a long hug. He reached out and flicked the wall switch, then picked her up and walked out of the dark kitchen. She continued crying softly even after they were undressed and in bed. Duke held her to his chest and stroked her hair until she finally fell asleep. He felt as if he were hurting her in some way he didn't understand.

"A toast to the beautiful *señorita!*"

The leader of the mariachi band lifted a mug of beer in salute. His fellow musicians whistled and raised their beers also. Shea, uncomfortable at being the center of attention, nearly blushed. Duke's friends had scrutinized her all evening, in a pleasant way, as if they'd already concluded that she would one day become Duke's wife. People crowded into the hacienda's courtyard and began to applaud. Duke's arm slid around her shoulders and her chest swelled with tenderness. He sensed her embarrassment and was trying to ease it.

"Gracias," she called cheerfully, nodding to the band members. She glanced up at Duke, and he winked as he raised his glass. Smiling, he bent his head and whispered several intimate words of praise in her ear.

"Your flattery has got to stop," she whispered back. "In about a hundred years."

O'Malley, looking very different to Shea because he wore slacks and a sport shirt instead of the grubby work clothes he'd favored in Mendocino, raised a glass and called out, "Here's to the Mendocino Group Home! A helluva proud project!"

The party crowd whistled and applauded again. As Shea raised her glass she turned her face away from Duke so that he wouldn't see her pensive expression.

The mariachi band started playing again. A pair of cowboy types with handlebar mustaches swaggered up, and Duke removed his arm from her shoulders to return their handshakes.

Shea took the opportunity to slip through the crowd and head inside. O'Malley caught up with her in Duke's huge airy kitchen as she traded her sangria for a glass of water.

"I've brought me Irish intuition with me tonight," he said in a terrible fake brogue. "And I think, me girl, that you're not very happy."

"O'Malley, you've got a lot of blarney, not intuition, and I'm fine." She patted his arm.

"You look fine, I admit it." He nodded at the flowers in her upswept hair, her white, off-the-shoulder top, and brightly colored skirt. "Like an ad for the Mexican tourist bureau."

Shea was proud of the outfit, prouder still that Duke had chosen it for her. She smiled. "It was a present."

"He adores you, lady. Everyone here has noticed it."

"The feeling's mutual."

"Is everything all right up in Mendocino? Duke said the first two weeks were rough, but he expects the next group of teenagers to be less trouble."

"They're girls, so he thinks that they'll be easy to manage. I haven't had the heart to tell him that he's wrong."

"Is that why you're so subdued tonight?"

"Relax, O'Malley, we only got here yesterday, and the trip's a long one. We have to head back to Mendocino tomorrow, and I've got a lot of paperwork waiting for me Monday morning. I'm just preoccupied."

Jennie wandered into the kitchen and thumped O'Malley on the arm before he could ask anything else. "I want to dance," she said firmly.

He grinned at her. "Don't mince words. Tell me exactly what you want, Red." He pivoted, grabbed her, and swung her around.

Shea smiled as she watched the two of them. Jennie's vacation had begun on Friday, and she'd left immediately for O'Malley's San Diego home. After the party they were heading for a resort on the Mexican coast. As far as Shea could tell, their relationship was passionate and good-natured but hardly serious.

"Vamoose," she told them.

Shea left the kitchen and went to the deep, sheltering porch that fronted the house, where she stood quietly, letting the night breezes play over her face and bare shoulders. The exterior of the house was white stucco, with a red tin roof, big deep-set doors, thick walls, and massive concrete columns that held up the porch. It was a study in reds and sun-bleached whites.

She loved Duke's place, with its amazing vista of sky and rolling, harsh land. The ranch was a green island carefully preserved by irrigation; somehow that made it more beautiful. Duke had fought hard to build something special in this dry, demanding section of the state.

When she heard footsteps behind her on the tile floor, she sensed that the long, confident stride could only belong to him. Shea turned to watch him walk toward her in the shadowy light.

"*Querida?*" he asked softly. "Are you feeling all right?" He cupped her face in his hands and tried to see her expression.

Shea kissed him lightly. "I'm having a terrific time. I'm just in a quiet mood."

That didn't satisfy him. "You've been that way for more than a week."

"Life has been, well, different lately. With the group home opening, and the kids coming over to the estate . . ."

"It'll settle down. Whatever's bothering you, tell me."

After a moment she admitted, "I'm not looking forward to the next group of teenagers."

He took her in his arms. "Palomino, I know they remind you of yourself as a teenager. Don't let the past hold on to you. You're a classy, successful woman, not a disadvantaged kid anymore. Let it go."

"I will, Alejandro. I just need time." The sounds of a slow, erotic song drifted to them from the courtyard. Shea felt as though the music were winding through her body. She put her head on Duke's shoulder and swayed slightly. He picked up the cue and moved with her. Their dance was barely more than an excuse to hold each other in the darkness.

Dawn widened the horizon with pink and magenta shadows as Duke guided Outlaw up the ridge. He glanced over at Shea, who had changed from her party outfit to jeans and a pullover sweater. With her face raised to catch the morning breeze, her rein hand relaxed on the horn of her saddle, she seemed at ease on the tall gray mare Luís had selected for her.

"It's been a while since I stayed up all night," she said. "This is a beautiful way to end a party."

"*Sí.* From loud to quiet. I like this better." They topped the ridge, and Outlaw stopped automatically. Shea's mare stopped alongside him.

"Oh, Alejandro." Shea's voice held wonder as she gazed at the distant desert. "It reflects the colors from the sunrise. It's like a dream."

"I've wanted to show you this place for a long time," he murmured. He dismounted and lifted her down from her horse.

"How old-fashioned and gallant," she whispered tenderly.

She put her arm around his waist, and he drew her close to his side. They stood silently for some time, watching the dawn melt the line between sky and desert.

Shea kissed his cheek and he turned to face her, his eyes intense, searching. He grasped both her hands. They looked at each other without moving.

"Will you marry me?" he asked.

Visions of a wonderful future with him flashed through her mind, igniting elemental emotions that she didn't need to analyze. She had known for a long time that she wanted to spend the rest of her life with Alejandro. Shea kissed him slowly, savoring him as if they'd never kissed before. She murmured her answer across his parted lips.

"Someday, sweetheart, of course."

He smiled quickly, then frowned. "Someday? I meant soon."

Shea shook her head and closed her eyes, trying to ease the knowledge that she was causing him pain. "No. Not right away."

He took her shoulders between his big hands as if he might shake her. "Someday is a lousy answer. Do you want to marry me or not?"

"Don't do this," she begged softly. "Don't be angry because I didn't say yes."

"But why . . . ?"

"I love you." She looked at him with pain showing in her eyes. "But I want to come to terms with my past. I'm unhappy, and I don't want to marry you when I feel this way. I want to know exactly who I am—past, present, and future. You encouraged me to begin this process, Alejandro. I'm glad."

"I brought this unhappiness into your life," he said wearily, "with the group home."

"Yes. But it's good for me, Alejandro."

He grimaced as if he, too, were hurting inside. "I'll

close the road to the estate and keep the teenagers away. I don't want you to be miserable."

"No. I'm not going to run from memories anymore."

The torment in his eyes made him look fierce. "But don't run from *me* either."

She caressed his face gently, trying to smooth away the concern and disappointment there. "I couldn't," she whispered. "You're part of my soul." She put her arms around his neck and held him almost desperately. "I'm sorry I've hurt you," she said raggedly. "Be patient, Alejandro. And never forget that I adore you."

With a muffled groan that conveyed both love and bittersweet frustration, Duke buried his face in her golden hair.

Nine

"Hello, ladies. Welcome to Estate Mendocino."

The looks Shea received for her polite words ranged from sullen to awed. Ten teenage girls stood in the reception area outside her office, accompanied by a female counselor from the group home. All wore shorts and lightweight tops, but uniformity ended there. Several of the girls resembled discount versions of Madonna, a couple were dressed in clothes three sizes too large, and the rest had discovered their own ways to proclaim their individuality.

Shea's eyes were drawn repeatedly to the most hostile of the group, a chubby brunet who wore a huge Los Angeles Rams football jersey, cutoffs, and unlaced basketball shoes. The girl had ancient green eyes in a face that could have been pretty except for its perpetual scowl. Her hair was shoulder length and shaggy. There was something about the girl's attitude that made Shea's insides churn with recognition.

Taking a deep breath, Shea plunged onward. "We're glad to have you as our guests here at Estate Mendocino, one of the finest health resorts in the world."

"Yeah, sure, you're glad to have us," muttered the brunet. "And Princess Di wants to invite us to tea too."

Shea decided it was pointless to continue the niceties. "Save the wisecracks for your first comedy spot on TV. I'm taking you guys to visit the estate's personal-design studio. In other words, we're spending the morning in the beauty parlor. Beauty is only skin deep, but self-image goes straight to the bone. Anybody who wants a make-over can have one. Anybody who doesn't can go swimming. Any questions?"

"I don't want a make-over, and I don't want to go swimming," the brunet retorted.

"Then read a magazine," Shea told her.

"I hate to read."

"Yeah," someone interjected, "she's too busy eating to have time to read."

The brunet turned menacingly toward the source of that comment and gave her some inventive instructions about her anatomy. Shea rubbed her forehead and grimaced. She hadn't heard this kind of crude repartee in years, and she'd forgotten how creative girls could be with words like those. She waved one hand toward the hallway.

"If you please, ladies. Beauty awaits."

The brunet sat morosely in a corner, watching the other girls get makeup and hair styling advice from the studio director and her assistants. The brunet was doing her best to give the impression that she wouldn't mind if the whole world went to hell. Shea's sympathies were drawn to her aggression and isolation, and she had the uncanny feeling that she'd known this girl all her life. She walked over and sat down beside her.

"I'm fourteen, my name's Amanda, and no, I don't want to make friends," the girl told her bluntly.

"I'm twenty-nine, you already know my name, and I don't want to make friends either." Shea suppressed a victorious smile when the girl looked at her askance. "I just want to talk. I'm as bored with this as you are."

"You? Hell, lady, you look like you spend half your day in joints like this."

"Wrong, but I'll take that as a compliment."

"I don't need this makeup and hair crap. I like myself the way I am." Amanda squinted at her angrily. "And I don't mind being fat, so don't do a psychology job on me. 'Poor little defensive fat kid.' "

"Great. Let's blow this joint and go swimming."

"Don't try to talk cool, lady. It's like watching Mary Poppins try to break dance. Unbelievable."

"I'm not as G-rated as I look. Now what about that swim?"

"I said before that I don't like to swim."

"All right, I'll bite. What do you like to do?"

"Pick up men and drink beer."

Shea didn't believe it for a minute. Yesterday she'd watched this girl cringe like a frightened rabbit when Duke introduced himself at the stables. She was afraid of people, men in particular.

"Picking up men and drinking beer sounds interesting," Shea responded.

"You never picked up a guy in your life, Goldilocks. And I bet you don't drink anything but champagne."

"I've developed a fondness for Mexican beer. And tequila."

"Yeah, and I'm Meryl Streep."

"Now there's a fascinating comment. Are you interested in acting?"

"Maybe." Her eyes lit with enthusiasm for a brief moment, as if a dark curtain had parted to allow light through. The curtain closed quickly. "Hey, I don't have to talk to you."

"Who said otherwise?"

Amanda twisted in her chair and looked resolutely stubborn. "I was forced to come to this stupid place, but I don't have to like it. Or you."

"Who forced you to come here?"

"My mother." Amanda smiled thinly. "The social worker told her it'd be good for me, and Ma never misses an opportunity to do what's good for me. 'Specially since she doesn't give a damn if I'm around or not."

The green eyes suddenly filled with tears. Shea's throat closed with a sympathy that went much deeper than Amanda could know, and she laid a soothing hand on the girl's arm. Amanda jumped as if she'd been burned with hot metal.

"Don't touch me," she snarled. "Keep your freaking manicured hands to yourself." A tear slid down her cheek and she brushed it away roughly. "Where's the john around this place?"

"That way." Shea pointed toward an exit, and the girl leapt up. "Amanda, it's okay . . ."

"Nothing's okay," Amanda shot back, and, one hand covering her face, ran from the room.

Prince Shalukan was rewriting the American Revolution. His armada of British gun ships menaced the city of Miami, which was represented by half a grapefruit he'd placed on the edge of the pool in his cottage.

"This would have changed the whole war," he told Duke and Shea excitedly. The prince, a stocky, dark-haired little man wearing bright-print bathing trunks, waded from one side of the pool to the other, arranging his miniature fleet. "You see, the British would have taken Miami, and then the French would have—"

"Whoa, Your Highness," Duke interjected politely, "there's one thing wrong."

The prince looked at Duke, then at Shea, his expression quizzical. Shea nearly strangled on repressed laughter because she didn't want to offend him. *Please, Alejandro, tell him what's wrong with his battle. I can't do it with a straight face.*

"Is a good military plan, yes?" the prince asked.

Duke nodded solemnly. "Oh, the plan's brilliant. Only catch is, the city of Miami didn't exist back then."

The prince gasped. "You are joking!"

"Afraid not, Your Highness. There were only a few towns on the Florida coast at the time of the Revolutionary War, and Miami wasn't one of them."

"My son, he tells me the wrong history! I send him to school in America, and he still gets things all wrong!"

Shea pointed to the grapefruit. "Let's change Miami to Boston. We'll cut an orange in two and make one half Philadelphia and the other half New York. Then—"

"Oh, shoo," the prince said with mild disgust. "We call it quits for the night. My mood is gone and my skin is wrinkling from too much water." He climbed out of the pool and his valet hurried to put a plush blue robe around his shoulders.

Duke stood and helped Shea to her feet. Prince Shalukan bowed to them, and they bowed back. "Thank you for being my audience," he told them. "I shall gladly extend a favor in return. Good night. I must go watch Johnny Carson."

When Duke and Shea were some distance away from the prince's cottage, they began to laugh. Clasping his side, Duke finally managed to drawl, "The British are coming, the British are coming! Close the beaches! Hide the plastic flamingos! Call Don Johnson!"

Shea covered her mouth with both hands to keep from whooping out loud. She leaned against Duke weakly, gasping for breath, and he slipped an arm around her shoulders.

"I'm glad to see you happy tonight, *querida*," he said tenderly. "I'm sorry that you were upset about that kid with the attitude problem."

Shea had told him at dinner about the scene with Amanda. Now she rested her head against Duke's chest and grew pensive. "I *know* that girl, Alejandro. We've just met, but I have a feeling that she and I are very much alike."

They walked slowly along the path toward her cottage. She wore a yellow strapless sundress, and he stroked her bare arm in a soothing way. "Palomino, don't be too openhearted for your own good. You're nothing like that troubled kid."

"I used to be," she murmured under her breath.

"Hmmm?"

"Nothing." Shea paused. "She compared me to Mary Poppins and Goldilocks."

Duke chuckled. "She's got the name of *that* tune." When Shea thumped his chest in rebuke, he added quickly, "Don't be insulted. I like you that way. I like you the other way too."

"What way is that?"

"When you're a wild mustang."

"Stop, I'm getting identity problems. Goldilocks, Mary Poppins, a wild mustang . . ."

"I'd like to get in bed with the mustang tonight."

Shea made a soft whinnying sound. As they reached her cottage door, she suddenly clasped her hand to her head. "Alejandro, I forgot to tell you. Sally Rogers called today to let us know that she's going to visit Jason regularly at his foster home."

Duke chuckled in delight. "Really? I think they're

perfect for each other—a big mouth and a bad mouth. I say that with affection on both counts."

Shea opened the cottage door and led the way inside. "You have to admit that not all of the estate's guests are selfish snobs," she told him firmly.

"One out of one hundred and twenty-three. Not good bettin' odds," he teased. The cottage was dark, and she made her way carefully toward a lamp. Suddenly Duke grabbed her from behind and ran both hands over the front of her sundress, squeezing her breasts. She uttered small sounds of encouragement, and Duke's voice dropped to a husky, rakish tone. "But the odds for my getting you naked and excited are *real* good, I'd say."

Shea felt the heat begin to build inside her body and silently blessed his loving instincts. He always seemed to know when a rowdy approach suited her mood. They would tumble into bed, barely taking time to remove all their clothes or sometimes without even accomplishing that task. But tonight she felt like prolonging the wildness.

"Let's play strip poker again," she challenged.

"Hmmm, you love it when I talk poker terms to you." He nibbled at her ear and whispered, "Aces high. My ace is already high."

Her stomach tumbled deliciously at his teasing innuendo. Shea snuggled closer and pressed her rump into the tops of his thighs. "Oh, Alejandro," she said with a sigh, "you're not bluffing."

They both groaned in dismay when the living-room phone rang. "Don't answer," he ordered gruffly, running his hands down her stomach.

"When I get a call at night, it's usually something important." He let go of her reluctantly, and she hurried to the phone on her coffee table. "Hello?"

Duke switched on a lamp by the couch and watched her expression become anxious as she listened to the caller. "Oh, no. *No*. He's right here. Wait a second." She held the phone out to Duke, her eyes full of worry. "It's the group home. Amanda has disappeared."

"Amanda! Amanda! It's Shea Somerton! If you can hear me, please say something!"

The redwoods were majestic giants that made the flashlight beams seem like pinpoints. Shea swung her light in an arc that crossed and recrossed with the lights of the five people who accompanied her. Ron, one of the estate's gym instructors, sighed loudly.

"She must have really been upset to run away before dinner," he muttered. "From what I heard, the fat kid never missed a meal in her life."

Old wounds opened inside Shea, fresh and agonizing. The pain combined with her concern for a girl who reminded her of her younger self, and she came to a rigid halt. Everyone else stopped too as she shone her flashlight into the staffer's startled face.

"Ron," she said in a hoarse whisper, "if I ever hear you make a cruel remark like that again, I'll fire you."

The other search parties were already back at the group home when she and her companions returned. All the lights shone in the main house, and Duke stood in the center of a crowd on the porch. His dark gaze rose over people's heads as her party walked out of the forest, and he left the porch to come to her. Shea shook her head as he put a hand on her shoulder.

"Nothing?" he asked gently.

"Nothing."

They walked back to the porch, where people were helping themselves to drinks and sandwiches brought from the estate. Duke handed her a cup of coffee. "Chug down every bit of that caffeine," he ordered.

"Yes, *hombre*."

The cup quivered visibly in her grip, and his expression tightened with concern. "Relax, *querida*, the police will find her."

Shea looked at him in surprise. "Do you mean you're turning the search over to them?"

"That's the way these things are handled, Shea. Runaways are an expected part of the routine in counseling programs like this. Hell, I ran away from more than one group home."

"And what happened?"

"The counselors called the police, the police found me, and I spent a night in jail. Then I was either sent back to Grandpa or to the group home."

"I don't want Amanda to be picked up by the police. It would terrify her."

"That kid's been in scrapes before. You read her history. I think she's as tough as buffalo hide."

"She's not. I know her better than you do."

He frowned, looking impatient. "Shea, stop overreacting. You just met the kid."

"I'm going to find her. I can't believe you're so unconcerned." Shea knew her voice was sharp, but she didn't care. She felt as if she were defending herself, not Amanda. In a way she was. No one, not even Duke, understood why she could empathize so well with the girl.

His eyes narrowed and the skin tightened on his face, making the scar on his nose more vivid. Shea gazed up at him staunchly. His expression would have cowed anyone but her.

"We've done all we can do," he said in a low, controlled voice. "I'm not unconcerned, I'm practical. This kid will make it to the road eventually, and the police will spot her."

"Dammit, stop calling her 'this kid.' She's a human being, and she needs my help."

She had never spoken to him so curtly before, and his reaction was swift. Disbelief shadowed his features for a moment, and then he grasped her upper arm with a slow, firm movement of his hand. The careful pressure of his fingers against her skin warned that he had been pushed too far. Duke bent his head and spoke so that no one else could hear.

"I don't know what the hell is wrong with you, but it's a little late for this self-righteous act. It doesn't come across as sincere."

His words struck her so harshly that she rested a trembling hand over the dull ache that squeezed her stomach. "You asked me to get involved," Shea told him in a choked, furious voice. "You wanted me to bleed for these kids." And because a cruel past was closing in on her, blotting out reason, she added raggedly, "You're lucky that I don't hate you for that."

"My *God*," he murmured, stunned.

Shea replayed her thoughtless words and felt as if she were freezing inside a cold chamber. The darkest pain glimmered in his eyes, and his fingers dug into her arm as he struggled for composure. She tried to talk, to say that she'd do anything to take the words back. What had she just done to Alejandro, she wondered in despair.

As Shea gazed up at him in mute sorrow, a sergeant from the county police stepped to her side. "Ms. Somerton, I heard one of your staffers say that you're upset. Don't worry, we'll find the girl." Shea nodded and numbly switched her gaze to the officer. "This area is so rural," he continued, "that there aren't too many places she can get to on foot. She might even come back to the group home eventually."

"Thank you, Sergeant."

The officer looked around. "This is some kind of interesting search party you've organized. I've never seen so many Rolex watches and diamond rings in my life. Tell them to go get some sleep. And you do the same."

Shea shook her head. "I can't."

"She will," Duke interjected icily.

Shea jerked her gaze back to him and read the determination in his fierce expression. Angry, Duke was formidable. But she had done more than make him angry; she had hurt him so deeply that the wound might never heal. In his pain, he was incapable of compromise. The sergeant murmured good night and walked away. Shea continued to stand immobile under Duke's bitter gaze.

"Stay here," he said, nearly whispering in his effort to control his emotions. "When I come back, we're going to have a *long* talk."

He pivoted stiffly and followed the sergeant. Shea watched him tell the counselors, the estate staff, and the guests that the police were taking over now, and he thanked them for their help. She couldn't take her eyes off his rigid back and proudly raised head; his anguish flowed straight to her and she wanted to cry.

But she knew what she had to do, and she could only pray that he would understand. She left the porch and slipped away in the darkness just as quietly as Amanda had.

He'd find her, and when he did, he'd tie her across his saddle like a captured slave. She deserved that for putting him through hell.

The black gelding Duke rode was accustomed to the mild demands of the estate's guests, not the hard riding of a master horseman. Sweating, snorting in dismay, the gelding angled through the trees at a lope, and only Duke's expert guidance kept both of them

from injury. Without the dawn light, Duke's reckless-
ness would have been even more dangerous.

When he saw the rocky landmark, Duke turned off
the trail and urged his tired mount up the steep, famil-
iar hill. "I'll let you rest in a minute, partner," he told
the horse in Spanish, and the rough compassion in
his voice encouraged the gelding to climb faster.

They topped the ridge, and Duke leaned forward as if
he could already see the small glen through the trees.
Let her be there. Please. He'd searched everywhere
else.

Shea was huddled on the steps, looking almost un-
real in the ethereal half-light. She had drawn up one
knee and rested her forehead there, cushioned on her
arm. A flashlight lay beside her. As Duke recognized
the exhaustion and despair in her posture, he nearly
forgot his anger.

His horse snorted as he reined it to a halt, and Shea
picked her head up. Duke climbed down from the saddle, and she stood to face him. Her jogging shoes were
muddy and unlaced, her jeans had ripped places at
the knees, and the forest's sharp fingers had ruined
the light knit top she wore. Her hair hung in a limp
blond ponytail. She held up both hands in a warning
gesture.

"I know you're upset with me, Alejandro, but I had to
keep looking for her. Please don't start an argument.
I've been walking around the forest all night, every
muscle in my body is tired, and I'm cold. I'm just
resting for a minute." As he strode toward her, his face
grim, she sensed his intentions and began backing up.
"You're not taking me back! I'm not stopping!"

"The hell you aren't. You're making yourself sick." He
continued in a torrent of Spanish, telling her exactly
what he thought of her stubborn and thoughtless
nature.

Shea nearly fell down as she stumbled against the cold, wet pipe that gurgled spring water. She stopped backing up and pointed at Duke accusingly. "I *do* care about the kids you brought to the estate! I care too much! Can you understand now? Amanda is *me*! I don't have to know her very well to know exactly what she's going through! You did this to me, Alejandro. Now let me handle it my own way!"

"Stop telling me that you and that teenager are just alike. Sympathy is one thing, but I'm fed up with your ridiculous self-torture." He pulled her by both wrists and seared her with a fierce, unhappy look. "Go ahead and hate me,' he said hoarsely. Duke hauled her toward him, then bent forward and braced one big shoulder against her stomach. The air whooshed out of her as he stood, hoisting her over his back as easily as he would a sack of horse feed.

Blood rushed to Shea's head and made her see pinpoints of light. She clutched the waist of his jeans and hung on grimly as he carried her to his horse. When he sat her down she shoved him away and unleashed her own emotional speech in Spanish.

"It's not love that makes you come looking for me! It's the need to be a bully! A *matón*, yes!"

"Tapar la boca."

"Be quiet? Is that the way you want me? Quiet . . . and docile?"

"I'd settle for quiet," he retorted. "I'm taking you back to your cottage." Then he turned her around to face his horse's saddle, grabbed the bottom of her rump with both large hands, and boosted her upwards. She threw one leg over the horse and landed with a jar that hurt every overworked joint in her body. Suddenly light-headed from nerves and exhaustion, she bent forward and rested her head on the horse's mane.

Alarmed, Duke touched his fingers to her pale, cool cheek. "Shea?"

She caught a sobbing sound in her throat. "Take me to the Japanese garden. It's the last place I can think of to look."

"No." He jerked his hand away and cursed viciously.

"I'll go without you! I don't need your help!"

"I don't think you need me at all. I don't know what you need." She started to sit up, but he reached out swiftly and anchored a hand on her shoulder. "I'll take you, dammit," he said raspily.

Duke put a foot in the stirrup and swung up behind her. His lower body crowded her rump, forcing her to sit up and scoot forward in the saddle. He slid one muscular forearm around her waist and trapped her against his powerful torso. His face was close to her ear and she could hear his rough breathing.

"I'll take you to the damned garden," he repeated. "And then I'll take you home. I'm leaving for the ranch after that."

Shea moaned softly. "No," she whispered in a distraught tone. "I didn't mean to—"

"You want to go to the garden? Then don't talk to me. I've heard enough."

Shea bit her lip and silent tears slipped down her face. They fell on his hand holding the reins, but he ignored them.

Instinct told Shea that should Amanda wander into the garden, she would linger there, mesmerized. Early morning was the prettiest time of day, when sunlight glinted off the ornate little pavilion and dew shimmered like spun silver on the exotic flowers. Their fragrances mingled with the rich earth scent of the surrounding forest, and hummingbirds floated among the blossoms.

So when Shea and Duke crested the hill and stopped, she half expected the scene they found—Amanda sitting on a stone bench by one of the garden's ornamental pools. She had her head bowed, and she didn't move. Her attitude conveyed a weariness and dejection that Shea understood intimately.

"So I was right," Shea whispered. "I should have looked here first."

Duke got down from the saddle, grasped her around the waist, and lifted her off the gelding. When her feet touched the ground, Shea turned to look up at him beseechingly. "Please," she said softly, a world of apology in the word.

He eyed her grimly. "We'll talk later."

Defeat drained her of argument and she simply nodded, then turned toward the garden. When Shea started down the curving stone steps, Duke grasped her arm. "Move easy, Palomino. She might spook and run."

Shea shook her head, and her eyes never left Amanda. "No, she won't run."

She continued down the steps, and Duke stayed beside her, his hand still holding her arm in case she stumbled from fatigue. But when he glanced at her face he saw strength and energy. She moved with unhurried grace, and as he watched, it seemed to him that her eyes filled with deep contentment. A startling idea came to him. *She hadn't just found the girl. She'd found herself.*

"Amanda?" Shea called.

The girl lifted her head and gaped at them in shock, then straightened defensively and slung her shaggy brunet hair away from her face. Her faded gray sweatshirt was rumpled, and a leaf clung to the leg of her blue jeans. Her fierce and haughty expression couldn't hide the evidence of dried tears.

"Yeah. You've found me. So what? I knew I'd get caught soon. I wasn't trying to hide, see?"

Shea sat down cross-legged on the stone floor by the bench and looked up at the girl calmly. Amanda stared back at her. Duke moved a few feet away and stood with his hands shoved in the front pockets of his jeans. "You look like hell," Amanda said abruptly, and jabbed a finger at Shea.

"I've been out in the woods all night, trying to find you."

"Why? You get bored with doing your nails and decide to play good fairy?" Amanda cut her eyes in Duke's direction. "No, I got it. You're just trying to impress *him*. You did it to make him happy."

Shea smiled, completely unrattled, and shook her head. "I did it for you. And for myself."

"Yeah, for yourself, right. What do you care about a fat kid with problems?"

Shea took a deep breath, shut her eyes for a moment, then locked her gaze on Amanda's. "I used to be a fat kid with problems."

After a stunned moment, Amanda uttered a terse obscenity that indicated her disbelief. "You don't have anything in common with *me*," she insisted.

"I've read your background. I grew up in an inner-city housing project, just like you did."

Amanda's mouth curved in a sneer. "Oh, yeah, and how did your mother make a living?"

Shea resisted a sudden gnawing urge to look at Duke. *Please understand, Alejandro*, she prayed silently. "She was a prostitute. Just like your mother. She was a waitress in a strip bar, and she sold herself to make extra money."

Amanda simply stared at her. Then her expression

tightened in a painful grimace that was part belief and part hope. "*You* came from *that*?"

Shea nodded. She glanced at Duke as he sat down on his boot heels. He had his head bent, and he jammed one hand through his hair. He was upset, either horrified or sympathetic or both. Shea struggled to clear the knot of fear from her throat and looked quickly back at Amanda.

"I don't even know who my father is," Shea continued. "I grew up poor, and overweight, and very, very angry at the world. If it hadn't been for a tough little woman who lived in our apartment building, I'd probably be—Lord knows what right now. She kept me out of serious trouble."

"I can't picture you in any kind of trouble, Goldilocks."

Shea smiled grimly. "By the time I was twelve, I was a terrific pickpocket and shoplifter. My best heist was a frozen turkey from a neighborhood grocery store."

"What the hell did you want with a frozen turkey?"

"It was Christmas, and the woman I mentioned—the one who kept me out of trouble—couldn't afford a turkey. So I brought her one. Unfortunately, she figured out that I stole it, and she made me take it back."

"But how . . . how . . ." Amanda waved one hand around her, indicating the estate. "How'd you end up running a fancy joint like this?"

"When I was fifteen, my mother got arrested. The state juvenile authorities decided I'd be better off in a foster home while she was serving time. I got lucky. Have you ever heard of *Funny Money*, that game show on television?"

"Sure. It's been around forever."

"The man who hosts it—he and his wife don't have any children of their own—so they take in foster kids. I went from living in public housing to living in a Beverly Hills home."

Duke spoke then, his voice low and incredulous. "Chip Greeson?"

Shea cleared her throat and stared down at her rigidly clasped hands. "That's right. I've always kept quiet about it because Chip's a celebrity. He and his wife don't want the press to find out about their work with foster children: Too much publicity would be hard on the kids. I lived with the Greesons until I was eighteen. I lost fifty pounds, I learned to like school, and I realized that I was a lot more than a prostitute's daughter. Later, the Greesons paid my way through college."

Amanda buried her face in both hands. "I bet I know why you were a fat kid."

"I'll bet you do," Shea agreed softly.

"So nobody would touch you."

Shea inhaled with painful slowness. "That's right. If I made myself unappealing, the men who hung around my mother—"

"Would stop trying to bother you," Amanda finished. She raised her head. The anger and sarcasm were gone from her features. "It works. I know."

Shea sat beside her on the bench. She put her arms around Amanda, and they shared a look of eternal compassion. "You're not alone," Shea told her. "I'll help you."

The tears Amanda cried now were tears of relief. "I've never had anybody who gave a damn about me," she murmured brokenly.

"Neither did I at your age. And it's taken me a long time to really believe that anyone *could* care about me."

Amanda buried her head on Shea's shoulder and sobbed. Shea closed her eyes and cried too—for Amanda, for all the young people hurt by the ugliness in the world, and for herself. What did Alejandro think of his golden princess now? Eventually, when her courage was high, she lifted her head to look at him.

He was gone.

"Boss, I was so worried."

"I'm all right," Shea interjected wearily. "Have you seen or heard from Duke?"

"He's in your office."

Shea halted in mid-stride and stared at her closed office door. Her stomach felt as though it was tied in knots. "Did he say anything?"

"Said you found the girl. That you and she were in the garden talking things over. Said he had some business to do, and he wanted to use your phone."

"I'm going in. If anyone calls, take a message."

"Want me to let Duke know—"

"No. I'll surprise him," Shea said grimly.

Her energy renewed a bit, she strode to the door, opened it without knocking first, and stepped into her office. Duke sat at her desk, her gold-and-white pedestal phone looking ridiculously dainty in his hand. He wore dark, aviator-style sunglasses, and she couldn't tell anything about his emotions as he glanced up.

Shea shut the door hard, went to the guest chair in front of the desk, and sat on the edge of the seat. She couldn't see his eyes, but she could tell from the angle of his head that he was staring straight at her.

"Will you take care of that immediately, Bill?" Duke told someone on the phone. "I'll come down to San Diego and sign the papers within the next couple of days. Yeah, that fast. All right. *Gracias.* Bye." He hung up the phone.

"Making plans to leave?" Shea asked in a low, tense voice.

"Making plans to give you the estate. A surveyor will

be out this afternoon to set up a dividing line between the estate and the group home. You'll get the new land plan along with a deed—".

"I don't want a gift given out of pity!" she protested, her voice rising. Shea stood and glared down at him, hurt and confusion battling inside her.

He stood too, his body rigid with tension and his mouth grim. "Don't push me, *querida*. I can't argue with you right now. Go to your cottage and wait for me. We'll talk in a little while."

"If I own this place now—or *will* own it, soon—I'll tell *you* what to do! Now that you know what I come from, you won't expect me to be delicate about it, will you?"

"Get out," he told her evenly. "I said we'll talk later." Then he pivoted, kicked her desk chair out of the way, and went to one of the office windows. He braced his hands on the jambs and gripped the wood so fiercely that she could see muscles flex under his shirt.

Shea wandered numbly to the settee near him and sank down. "Say it," she rasped in a wretched tone. "Just say that you walked away because you were disgusted by what I told Amanda. You've always given me the truth before. Do it now."

He groaned softly and turned his head to look at her. "Woman, you get the wildest notions. I wasn't disgusted. I love you more than ever."

After a moment she managed to ask, "Then why did you walk away?"

Duke looked back out of the window, his jaw clenched, the sinews straining in his neck. "Dammit, Palomino, leave me alone for a little while, won't you?"

"I'm dying inside because I don't know what's in your mind right now, Alejandro! I'm not leaving this room!" She got up and went to him, grasped his arm tightly, and leaned her forehead on his shoulder. "Say it in Spanish, in English, in pig Latin, I don't *care*. Just tell me what you feel!"

He trembled beneath her hands. His voice was a low rasp. "Latin men are macho, *querida*. We don't like to cry in front of our women." He shifted, struggling for control as if he were forcing himself to lift an impossible weight.

Suddenly Shea understood why he'd left her alone with Amanda. Tenderness and relief sleeted through her, and she caught a sob in her throat.

"You left because you didn't want me to see you cry? Oh, Alejandro. It doesn't embarrass me. I don't think you're less of a man if you cry in front of me. You cried once when we were making love, remember?"

"A few tears from happiness. This . . . is different. And this morning I had . . . so many things to say to you. They were for you alone, so I walked away. The girl, is she . . ."

"She's asleep in a room here at the main house. She's fine." Shea hesitated. "I'm going to help her somehow. I'll have to talk to the authorities and see what can be done."

"*Sí*. We'll help her, *querida*." His deep voice was suddenly tinged with anger. "The way I would have helped you weeks ago, if you'd trusted me."

Shea stroked his back for a second, then murmured, "I trust you more than I've ever trusted anyone in my life."

He made a disdaining sound. "That's a hell of an accolade. You don't trust me enough, but it'll have to do, eh?" Before she could answer, he continued hoarsely, "I would have listened. I would have *cared*. And things between us would have been so much simpler, if you'd told me that you'd been abused as a kid."

Shea knotted her hands in his shirt and pressed her

forehead against his taut, unyielding back. "It's not the kind of story a woman enjoys telling her lover."

"I'm your friend as well as your lover. I have to know everything—what makes you uncomfortable, what scares you, what still has power over you."

She struggled for a moment, trying desperately to tear down the walls inside her, her hands clenching harder and her face contorted with pain. "Be my friend," Shea managed to say finally. "And don't ask me to talk about things that might disgust you."

He shifted as a shudder went through him. "If you don't talk, it will always be between us."

"Only if you concentrate on it."

"You're shutting me out. I can't stand that."

She began to cry. "No, no. I'm letting you *in*. Just as much as I possibly can. Don't you understand? There's still a part of me that feels dirty and ashamed. It's so ugly that I don't want to share it with anyone."

"Palomino," he whispered wretchedly. "There's nothing ugly about you. Come here." He angled his body and raised one arm, beckoning to her without turning around.

Shea slipped quickly to the front of him and buried her face against his chest. She shook with sobs as he put both arms around her in an embrace so possessive and tight that he seemed to be pulling her inside his soul. "Don't leave me," she begged.

His arms wound her even closer to him. "I couldn't," he whispered against her hair. "God help me, no matter what you refuse to tell me, I couldn't leave you. You ought to know that." His voice nearly broke. "You *ought* to, but you don't."

"Some day, Alejandro . . . some day I'll tell you everything."

He rested his cheek against her hair and said sadly, "That *some day* could ruin me, *querida*."

Ten

A few days later, when he handed her the deed to Estate Mendocino, Shea tore the document up and handed it back to him. He swore colorfully for a full ten seconds.

"You still feel sorry for me," she told him frankly. "You want to make up for every bad thing that ever happened to me. But you don't have to, Alejandro. I've never been happier than I am right now."

His mouth thinned and he looked exasperated. "You insult me, Palomino. Giving you the estate makes me feel as if I've done something to change what happened in your childhood. It makes me feel less angry. So, there! I have a selfish motive. If you want to make me happy, accept my gift."

Shea rubbed her forehead and pondered his logic. "*Hombre*, you're more confusing than the L.A. freeway during rush hour." She studied his determined expression. "We'll be partners," she said finally. "Have your attorney draw up the papers that way."

"You've always wanted full control over the fat farm. You know how it operates, you love it, you can run it with your eyes closed. It belongs to you in spirit already. Why won't you take it as a present?"

"I don't need to feel so protected anymore, Alejandro. I know that you won't sell the estate or do anything to harm it. I trust you. Let's be partners, fifty-fifty." She paused, thinking of the income involved. "I'll be rich!"

"Ah-hah, and then you'll buy mauve jogging suits trimmed in mink. You'll get a poodle and put bows in its hair. Who knows what else? I take the whole offer back!"

Smiling for the first time in several days, she tossed a poker chip at him. They faced each other across a patio table in the courtyard of his ranch house, playing cards and sharing swigs from a bottle of wine. She wore a silky white robe and he wore cut-off jeans. The day was fading into a brilliant orange sunset.

"I don't want mink or a poodle," Shea told him. "I want to buy an apartment building."

"Hmmm. So you want to be a landlord."

"I want to be a slumlord." When he gave her an astonished look, she added, "I want to buy something in Los Angeles and fix it up just for low income families. You know, give them a decent place to live for modest rent."

He thought for a moment, frowning. "Palomino, you're biting off more than you can chew. Why not contribute to some good charities, instead?"

"I want to do something more personal."

"Bake brownies for the group home, then."

"Alejandro! I never expected a cold comment like that from *you.*"

Duke was wearing his reading glasses. He pulled them down to the tip of nose and looked at her over the wire rims. "I don't like cities," he said bluntly. "Too dangerous. I'd prefer that you not make regular trips to a run-down part of L.A. to visit an apartment building."

"So that's your worry. I'll hire a good manager to handle everything—it's not as if I'd be involved in the day-to-day problems. Besides, I grew up in that area. I know how to take care of myself."

Duke studied her for a moment, thinking how incredibly beautiful she was, how classy. She had suffered so much as a child, yet survived to become this wise, compassionate person. She was a great lady in the gallant, old-fashioned sense of the words. In some ways she still thought of herself as poor and unattractive, and that was a problem. She couldn't believe that her sleek blond elegance would draw attention and trouble in a slum neighborhood.

"You don't understand, *querida*," he said in a soft somber voice. His eyes burned into her. "If someone hurt you, I'd kill him."

Shea stared at him for a moment, speechless. He was serious, and his vow had nothing to do with some macho code of honor, but rather with the simple fact that he loved her more than anything or anyone in the world.

"*Hombre*," she murmured, and gave him a teary, adoring look. "We'll talk about this later. I don't think you can change my mind."

Duke tossed his cards down. Frustration rose inside him, giving birth to the anger that stayed just beneath the surface now. "Buying the damned apartment building is a shield," he told her. "You can't dissolve your past by doing good deeds."

"It's one way," she protested softly, her voice strained.

"One way to bury memories that you ought to share with me."

Shea stiffened with misery. The light-hearted mood they had cultivated so carefully all day was fading with the sunset. "It's a simple thing, Alejandro. Don't analyze it. I want to help people."

"Help yourself, first. Help me by talking."

"There are times when I think you're the most stubborn, impatient man I've ever known."

He spread his hands in a gesture of futility. "What are you afraid of? That I'll be shocked by what you tell me? That I would blame you for a situation you couldn't control? That I want to learn more so that I can torture you with it?"

Swiftly, with a violence she didn't know she possessed, Shea slung a hand out and whipped their playing cards from the table. They fluttered in bright disarray to the courtyard's rust-red tiles. She stood, trembling, and glared down at him through furious tears. "Give me some peace!" she pleaded in Spanish. "You have no way of knowing what you'll feel, and neither do I! No more talk right now! When you can come to me without demands and anger, I'll be waiting!" Her taut expression crumpled in a look of abject sorrow as she swung around on one bare heel and went into the house.

Seconds later he heard a door shut heavily, and judged by the sound that she had secluded herself in the study near his bedroom. Duke grabbed the wine bottle they had shared moments earlier, threw it across the courtyard, and watched with narrowed eyes as it smashed into glittering pieces.

They took Amanda on a shopping spree at Giorgio's Beverly Hills boutique, then had lunch at a streetside cafe near the UCLA campus. When they settled once again in the Cadillac Duke had rented at the Los Angeles airport, they rode through Beverly Hills' palm-lined streets in silence.

"I cried the first time I came here," Shea finally admitted.

Amanda nodded fervently. "If the Greesons kick me out, I'm coming back to Mendocino."

"No one'll kick you out," Duke assured her. "Pretty soon you'll feel right at home."

"Good," Amanda noted. "It'd be nice to feel at home somewhere."

Her mother hadn't protested at all when they'd suggested that Amanda move into a foster home. Amanda hadn't been terribly hurt by her mother's reaction; it was typical. Arranging the move with the state juvenile authorities had been relatively simple.

When they reached their destination, a gardener opened a massive, wrought-iron gate and waved them through. "Double hell," Amanda said fearfully when she saw the 20-room, Tudor-style mansion surrounded by formal gardens. "I'll get lost going to the bathroom."

Amanda and her belongings were quickly installed in an upstairs bedroom. The Greesons had five other foster children, ranging in age from seven to fifteen, three girls and two boys. The hearty crew took Amanda on a tour of the house, and when Shea and Duke left, Amanda was learning to play backgammon.

Shea sat close to the passenger window and stared out silently as Duke drove away.

"Sad?" he asked.

"I'll miss her. But sad? No. I'm excited that she's going to have the same opportunities I had." She hesitated a moment. "I want to show you something this afternoon. In downtown L.A."

"Where?"

"Just follow my directions, *hombre*, and don't ask questions."

"Kidnapped," he muttered.

•   •   •

He figured out her scheme when he realized that she was heading them toward a run-down section of the city. Duke's mood turned black, but he said nothing. The summer sun seemed to be roasting Los Angeles under a covering of brown smog. The streets were treeless and gray, as if the life had been drained out of them. Trash littered the sidewalks, and the storefront windows were covered with bars.

"The exterior scenes for *Hill Street Blues* were filmed nearby," Shea said pleasantly.

Duke scowled. "A great recommendation."

"I suppose you know why I wanted to come here."

"To look at an apartment building. Dammit, Shea—"

"Just keep an open mind."

The building's simple angular design marked its age at about thirty years. The exterior was white concrete block, but neighborhood graffiti artists had decorated the lower level with a variety of slogans, some of them obscene. The building stood three stories tall. It was centered on a small lot where a few tufts of grass and scraggly box shrubs struggled to survive.

Duke parked on the street next to a crumbling walkway that led to the building's front doors. A dark-haired boy, probably no more than ten years old, walked up immediately and pointed to the rental car. "Mister, you give me five bucks. I make sure no one rips you off." His voice was heavily accented, and Duke answered him in Spanish.

"Here's five bucks, *muchacho*, and there'll be five more if the radio and hubcaps are still here when I get back."

"*Sí.*"

Shea winced a little and avoided looking at Duke. He took her arm in a tight grip and they started up the walkway. She could almost feel his thoughts churning angrily.

They found the resident manager's apartment on the bottom floor. When Shea knocked, a tall skeletal old man came to the door. The wad of tobacco stopped moving in his cheek as he gave the two of them a startled once over. Duke suddenly wished that he'd worn jeans and a T-shirt instead of a sport jacket, golf shirt, and crisp tan slacks. Shea looked like rainbow sherbet in a raw-silk jacket, peach-colored slacks, and a pink silk top. They were both out of place.

"Yeah?" the man grunted.

"I'm Shea Somerton. The owner was supposed to tell you that I'd be here today."

"Yeah. What d'ya wanna know?"

"How many apartments are rented?"

"Fifteen. I got fifteen others vacant. They need to be fixed up 'fore anybody'll rent 'em. Second floor's all empty. Part of the third, too. Doors are unlocked in the vacant apartments."

"We'll just walk around the place, if that's okay."

"Sure. I don't give a damn."

"Thank you," Shea said politely. The man shut the door without answering.

Duke grimaced. "Son of a . . . Let's get out of this rat hole, *querida*."

"You promised to keep an open mind."

He looked at her for a moment, then beyond her to a narrow hallway with its dirty walls and stained floors. "If you want to look around, let's look," he said. "My mind's closing fast."

"I want to see the second story." They walked to a staircase at the back of the hallway. Duke angled in front of her and started up. "You don't have to run defense for me, Alejandro."

"Indulge my masculine pride." He kicked a fast-food wrapper aside with his foot. "How the hell did you find this place?"

They reached the landing of the second level. Distracted, Duke didn't realize that she hadn't answered. Shea pushed in front of him and pulled open the fire door that led to a hallway. He glanced at her face and saw that she was very pale except for small clouds of pink that colored her cheeks. She looked sick.

"Palomino . . ." he began anxiously, but she was already walking down the hallway.

Cursing, Duke strode after her. The apartment doors were painted a revolting shade of green. The hall carpet looked as if a herd of elephants had been quartered on it. She stopped near the end of the hall and gazed fixedly at the corroded metal number on one of the doors. She reached for the doorknob tentatively, as if she were afraid it might shock her.

"Oh, no, you don't," Duke said. He blocked her way with his arm and covered her hand on the doorknob. "Step back."

"It's just an empty apartment," she protested, a strained expression on her face.

"Except for rats and Lord knows what else."

She sighed, defeated. "I love you, Alejandro, even if you are a bully."

"Good."

She moved back several feet and watched him shove the door open. She saw torn floor covering, piles of boxes and rags, and a filthy mattress. A bare, dirty window framed the Los Angeles skyline in the distance.

"A real Taj Mahal," Duke noted grimly. He stepped into the apartment, put his hands on his hips, and gazed around. She walked in after him, her steps slow, her hands clasped in front of her.

"It used to be a good deal better than this."

He turned around, took a long look at the sorrowful expression on her face, and everything about her strange attitude clicked into place. "Dammit, Shea," he murmured tightly. "This is where you grew up. You look like you've just stepped inside a tomb."

She nodded wearily. "It is a tomb. There are a lot of memories buried in it."

They were both silent for a moment. Duke felt a little stunned. Finally he said grimly, "*Querida*, you should have told me that this was the building you wanted to buy." He ran a hand through his hair and shook his head in disgust. "One more secret, one more thing you don't want to tell."

"I didn't know until a few days ago that it was for sale. When Mother and I lived here, it was owned by the city housing authority. I found out that the city sold it a few years ago. And now it's up for sale again."

Duke grimaced in self-reproach. "Forgive me for sounding like such a bastard." He went over and slipped an arm around her shoulders. She leaned against him as they walked through the small apartment. "This was mine," she told him when they stopped in a tiny, windowless room. Shea put a hand on a peeling strip of wallpaper and pulled it away to reveal the older wallpaper underneath. "I put that paper up myself. I must have been about twelve. I did a terrible job, but I thought it was beautiful."

Duke looked at the cheap, faded print and felt a poignant sorrow rise in his chest. "Roses," he said gruffly.

"Señora Savaiano helped me pick it out."

"She was the elderly woman who looked after you?"

"Yes."

They walked into another room, only slightly larger. It had a window, and several of the panes were broken. "Mother's room," Shea noted in a brusque tone.

Duke kissed her forehead, rested his cheek there, and shut his eyes. She was trembling, and he stroked her arm.

"She could have been beautiful," Shea murmured hoarsely. "And I loved her." She twisted abruptly and hid her face against his neck. Her voice was full of torment. "Let's sit down."

"Not here, *querida*."

"Here. It's the only place I can force myself to talk."

She pulled away from him, went back to the main room, and lowered herself gracefully to the floor, heedless of what the dirt would do to her outfit. She hugged her knees to her chest and stared at a point on the far wall. Duke followed and stood over her, watching desperate emotions flicker over her face.

This was the moment he'd demanded, but he felt no victory. "This isn't what I wanted," he said gently. "You don't have to surround yourself with pain."

"Yes, I do," she corrected. "I know that I have to stop shutting you out of my past." She paused, struggling hard to sound calm. "I love you so much, and I don't want to hurt you anymore."

"Sssh." He sat down behind her and began rubbing her shoulders. "It isn't me you're hurting, it's *us*."

She nodded, and her head drooped. Slowly, pulling the agony out of her mind like briars, she began to tell him how life had been. Minutes flowed away, carrying one excruciating story after another. Shea was dimly aware each time Duke's hands stopped moving on her shoulders, then gripped fiercely, then stroked in sympathy. She heard him make soft, harsh noises deep in his throat.

She was handing him her pain and humiliation and fear without any guarantee that he could bear it. "Do you want me to stop?" she asked raggedly.

"No." Suddenly his arms came around her from behind. "We're all right. Go on."

He rocked her while she talked, his body a warm, strong support. She cried; she unwound her arms from around her knees and shook clenched fists at everything that had happened to her in these squalid little rooms.

Two hours passed before she ran out of words and buried her face in her hands. Silence descended, punctuated by the distant sounds of children playing outside. Her nerves were raw as she waited for Duke to say something.

"It's over," he murmured, his voice low and soothing against her ear. "From now on, we can deal with it."

She nodded blankly. He was so calm—or was he merely assuming a careful facade to reassure her? Shea twisted to look at him. His face showed the exhaustion of his emotional turmoil. He kissed her tenderly, then got to his feet and helped her up, too.

Shea was terrified by his silence. Her throat raw, her heart pounding, she held his hand fiercely when they went downstairs, as if she were afraid that the bad aura of the place would hurt him somehow. She didn't have the courage to ask how he really felt about her now.

They left through a back exit and walked around the building. Dirty, half-dressed children stopped playing and stared at them with wide eyes. The tenants' laundry hung from clothes lines held by rickety supports.

"I'm going to put in a laundry room with washers and dryers," she noted.

"Hmmm. Good."

More fear poured into her veins as she analyzed his mood. Was it quiet acceptance, or shock? They walked farther. Suddenly Shea grabbed his arm and pointed toward the brown-tinged box shrubs at the base of the building. She uttered a strangled sound, ran to the shrubs, knelt on the dusty ground beside them, and pulled their bottom branches aside.

"Look, Alejandro. Oh, *look*," she said in a voice full of

bittersweet happiness. She pointed to a fist-size stump with a few sharp little leaves growing from the top.

Shea tilted her head back and studied him with a mixture of hope and despair. Had she found a beginning, or an end? Tears streamed down her face. "There's one left. One rose bush."

Duke reached out slowly and stroked tendrils of soft blond hair back from her forehead. "You see," he whispered hoarsely, "the beauty survives."

For several seconds, Shea looked at him in awe. Life stopped to let her savor the moment when fear fell away. He knew everything about her, and she was at his mercy. This was the threshold between darkness and light.

And she was leaving the darkness behind.

Quivering, she stood as gracefully as she could, her eyes never leaving his. Communicating was simple, she thought, when trust became this strong. It was difficult to compose herself, but Duke's eyes held nothing but patience. She had to speak the words properly, without her voice breaking.

"I love you more than you can ever imagine. Will you marry me?" she asked.

He tried to answer but couldn't manage it easily, so he simply held out both hands and nodded. She went into his arms and he lifted her off the ground when he kissed her. "Yes, and forever," he murmured afterward.

The sky over Mendocino was brilliantly blue on the day of their marriage, a cloudless winter day when sunshine etched the world in lines of crystal clarity. The small white church sat at the edge of town, facing the ocean. It had been built over a hundred years earlier of native redwood, in a beautifully simple style. A single steeple rose against the blue canopy of sky.

Shea peeked furtively out of the tiny room off the church vestibule. "Jennie! Help! The crown of this veil is so tall that I need a crane to put it on!" Jennie, who was adjusting O'Malley's black bow tie, turned to gaze at her with amusement. Shea gave O'Malley a hurried wave. "How's my man doing?"

"He's out in the parking lot teaching Jason how to palm coins. He says he's calm, but he's dropped his quarter five times already. I'll go check on him."

After O'Malley left, Jennie swept into the changing room and shut the door. "Sit down, boss, and let me have a whack at that strange gear." She smiled. "You look like the heroine of an old Zorro movie. Fantastic."

Shea brushed a fingertip across the bodice of her dress. "I hope that my Zorro thinks so."

Her Zorro did. It was obvious in the way he flashed an ecstatic smile when she appeared at the back of the aisle. She couldn't stop looking at him. He wore a black tuxedo with a red cummerbund and a brightly colored serape arranged over his right shoulder. The small church was lit only by candles and the afternoon light streaming through the western windows. The soft golden hues seemed to shimmer around him, as if someone had thrown gold dust into the air.

He presented a darkly exotic and very compelling picture, and she was breathless as she walked down the aisle alone, smiling at him the whole way. In her arms she carried a huge bouquet of mixed roses—every color and every type that had been available. Her dress was a miracle of meticulous reproduction, created from drawings of 19th-century Mexican styles. Delicate lace overlaid the slender sleeves and the tight bodice with its high, regal collar. The ivory satin skirt was so volu-minous that it brushed the pews on both sides of the aisle. Shea's veil trailed down her back from the tall crown set with pearls amid swirling, embroidered patterns.

Alejandro's dark eyes gleamed with pleasure when she stopped beside him. He took her hand in a warm, tight grip and seductively stroked her palm with the tip of his forefinger. His gaze was tender but also teasing. Despite the fact that the minister was about to begin and she shouldn't have kissed Alejandro until *after* the ceremony, she brushed her lips across his cheek. "*Hombre*," she whispered so that only he could hear.

Jason, more jaunty than ever because he'd just been adopted by Sally Rogers, was the ring bearer. At the appropriate moment in the proceedings he held his pillow out with one hand and gave them a thumbs-up with the other. Duke returned the gesture, and laughter rippled through the packed church.

At the end of the ceremony they shared what was most likely the longest wedding kiss in the history of Mendocino, and the guests broke into applause when they stopped. Duke wasn't content to let her simply walk out of the church by his side; he swooped her up in a cloud of lace and satin, then carried her down the aisle and out the door.

The mariachi band waiting at the bottom of the church steps burst into a lively tune. "Surprise!" Duke said, and she laughed as she planted quick, loving kisses all over his face. He set her down, stepped back, and bowed formally. "Señora Araiza," he said with great pride, then straightened and held out his arm. "Will you walk with me to the wedding reception?"

She curtsied. "Señor Araiza, I'd be most honored." They'd planned a feast at the Mendocino Hotel, just a few blocks away on Main Street. Shea took his arm and looked up at him with adoration. "But there's one thing I need to do first."

People came out of the church and crowded around them. Shea pulled a perfect red rose from her bouquet, then searched the crowd until she found Amanda and the Greesons.

"Ah, I think I understand," Duke murmured softly.

He let her go and watched as she walked to Amanda. They hugged, and Shea laid the rose in her hand. When she came back to Duke, her eyes glistened with tears and she was smiling.

"This is a very unusual way to end a wedding day, don't you think?"

"*Querida*, did you want a quiet, ordinary wedding day?"

"No," she admitted. "But I never expected to walk through the woods in jogging shoes and my wedding dress. I didn't expect to spend tonight in a roofless, half-finished house." Shea nuzzled his neck and curled a leg over his thighs. "But I *did* expect to make love with you. It was wonderful."

Duke chuckled and stroked her bare back. They lay naked under a pile of blankets on the floor of what would one day be a large living room—their living room—in a log-and-stone house centered on land between the estate and the group home. Duke's ranch would be their second home.

They gazed up through the bare rafters at a night sky filled with stars. "Think of all the years ahead of us," he whispered. "How many nights we'll watch the stars together."

"And how many nights I'll do this to you, sweetheart." She let her hand wander down his stomach.

"I can't concentrate on the stars if you do that."

"The stars will always wait."

"Hmmm. They'll have to, *querida*."

He pulled her across his body and held her tightly. Their slow, sweet merger added whispers of love to the night. They fell asleep afterward, and when they woke they watched the sun rise over forested hills.

"How about an early-morning mud bath?" Shea whispered against his ear.

He rose on one elbow and looked down at her with devotion and amusement. "I never thought I'd say this . . . but I'm going to enjoy taking mud baths with you for the rest of my life."

"Sí, hombre," she murmured, her eyes gleaming. "I'll make certain."

THE EDITOR'S CORNER

Next month's LOVESWEPTs are sure to keep you warm as the first crisp winds of autumn nip the air! Rarely do our six books for the month have a common theme, but it just so happens our October group of LOVESWEPTs all deal with characters who must come to terms with their pasts in order to learn to love from the heart again.

In **RENEGADE**, LOVESWEPT #282, Judy Gill reunites a pair of lovers who have so many reasons for staying together, but who are pulled apart by old hurts. (Both have emotional scars that haven't yet healed.) When Jacqueline Train and Renny Knight struck a deal two years earlier, neither one expected their love to flourish in a marriage that had been purely a practical arrangement. And when Renny returns to claim her, Jacqueline is filled with panic . . . and sudden hope. But with tenderness, compassion, and overwhelming love Renny teaches her that the magic they'd created before was only a prelude to their real and enduring happiness.

LOVESWEPT #283, **ON WINGS OF FLAME**, is Gail Douglas's first published romance and one that is sure to establish her as a winner in the genre. When Jed Brannen offers Kelly Flynn the job of immortalizing his uncle's beloved pet in stained glass, she knows it's just a ploy on Jed's part. He's desperate to rekindle the romance that he'd walked away from years before. He'd been her Indiana Jones, roaming the globe in search of danger, and she'd almost managed to banish the memory of his tender caresses—until he returns in search of the only woman he's ever loved. Kelly's wounded pride makes her hold back from forgiving him, but every time she runs from him, she stumbles and falls . . . right into his arms.

Fayrene Preston brings you a jewel of a book in **EMERALD SUNSHINE**, LOVESWEPT #284. Too dazzled by the bright blue Dallas sky to keep her mind on the road, heroine Kathy Broderick rides her bike smack into Paul Garth's sleek limousine! The condition of her mangled bike isn't nearly as important to Kathy, however, as the condition of her heart when Paul offers her his help—

(continued)

and then his love. But resisting this man and the passionate hunger she feels for him, she finds, is as futile as pedaling backward. Paul has a few dark secrets he doesn't know how to share with Kathy. But as in all her romances, Fayrene brings these two troubled people together in a joyous union that won't fail to touch your soul.

TUCKER BOONE, LOVESWEPT #285, is Joan Elliott Pickart at her best! Alison Murdock has her work cut out for her as a lawyer who finds delivering Tucker's inheritance—an English butler—no small task. Swearing he's no gentleman, Tucker decides to uncover Alison's playful side—a side of herself she'd buried long ago under ambition and determination. Alison almost doesn't stop to consider what rugged, handsome Tucker Boone is doing to her orderly life, until talk of the future makes her remember the past—and her vow to rise to the top of her profession. Luckily Tucker convinces her that reaching new heights in his arms is the most important goal of all!

Kay Hooper has written the romance you've all been waiting for! In **SHADES OF GRAY,** LOVESWEPT #286, Kay tells the love story of the charismatic island ruler, Andres Sereno, first introduced in **RAFFERTY'S WIFE** last November. Sara Marsh finds that loving the man who'd abducted her to keep her safe from his enemies is something as elemental to her as breathing. But when Sara sees the violent side of Andres, she can't reconcile it with the sensitive, exquisitely passionate man she knows him to be. Andres realizes that loving Sara fuels the goodness in him, fills him with urgent need. And Sara can't control the force of her love for Andres any more than he can stop himself from doing what must be done to save his island of Kadeira. Suddenly she learns that nothing appears black and white to her anymore. She can see only shades of gray . . . and all the hues of love.

Following her debut as a LOVESWEPT author with her book **DIVINE DESIGN,** published in June, Mary Kay McComas is back on the scene with her second book for us, **OBSESSION,** LOVESWEPT #287. A powerful tale of a woman overcoming the injustices of her past with the help of a man who knows her more intimately than

(continued)

any other person on earth—before he even meets her—Mary Kay weaves an emotional web of romance and desire. Esther Brite is known to the world as a famous songwriter, one half of a the husband and wife team that brought music into the lives of millions. But when her husband and son are killed in a car accident, Esther returns to her hometown, where she'd once been shunned, searching for answers to questions she isn't sure she wants to ask. Doctor Dan Jacobey has reasons of his own for seeking sanctuary in the town of Bellewood—the one place where he could feel close to the woman he'd become obsessed with—Esther Brite. Esther and Dan discover that together they are not afraid to face the demons of the past and promise each other a beautiful tomorrow.

I think you're going to savor and enjoy each of the books next month as if you were feasting on a gourmet six-course meal!

Bon appetite!

Carolyn Nichols

Carolyn Nichols
    Editor
LOVESWEPT
Bantam Books
666 Fifth Avenue
New York, NY 10103

THE HOMETOWN HUNK CONTEST

**FOR EVERY WOMAN WHO HAS EVER SAID—
"I know a man who looks
just like the hero of this book"
—HAVE WE GOT A CONTEST FOR YOU!**

To help celebrate our fifth year of publishing LOVESWEPT we are having a fabulous, fun-filled event called THE HOMETOWN HUNK contest. We are going to reissue six classic early titles by six of your favorite authors.

> **DARLING OBSTACLES by Barbara Boswell**
> **IN A CLASS BY ITSELF by Sandra Brown**
> **C.J.'S FATE by Kay Hooper**
> **THE LADY AND THE UNICORN by Iris Johansen**
> **CHARADE by Joan Elliott Pickart**
> **FOR THE LOVE OF SAMI by Fayrene Preston**

Here, as in the backs of all July, August, and September 1988 LOVESWEPTS you will find "cover notes" just like the ones we prepare at Bantam as the background for our art director to create our covers. These notes will describe the hero and heroine, give a teaser on the plot, and suggest a scene for the cover. Your part in the contest will be to see if a great looking local man—or men, if your hometown is so blessed—fits our description of one of the heroes of the six books we will reissue.

THE HOMETOWN HUNK who is selected (one for each of the six titles) will be flown to New York via United Airlines and will stay at the Loews Summit Hotel—the ideal hotel for business or pleasure in midtown Manhattan—for two nights. All travel arrangements made by Reliable Travel International, Incorporated. He will be the model for the new cover of the book which will be released in mid-1989. The six people who send in the winning photos of their HOMETOWN HUNK will receive a pre-selected assortment of LOVESWEPT books free for one year. Please see the Official Rules above the Official Entry Form for full details and restrictions.

We can't wait to start judging those pictures! Oh, and you must let the man you've chosen know that you're entering him in the contest. After all, if he wins he'll have to come to New York.

Have fun. Here's your chance to get the cover-lover of your dreams!

Carolyn Nichols

Carolyn Nichols
Editor
LOVESWEPT
Bantam Books
666 Fifth Avenue
New York, NY 10102–0023

THE HOMETOWN HUNK CONTEST

DARLING OBSTACLES
(Originally Published as LOVESWEPT #95)
By Barbara Boswell

COVER NOTES

The Characters:

Hero:
GREG WILDER's gorgeous body and "to-die-for" good looks haven't hurt him in the dating department, but when most women discover he's a widower with four kids, they head for the hills! Greg has the hard, muscular build of an athlete, and his light brown hair, which he wears neatly parted on the side, is streaked blond by the sun. Add to that his aquamarine blue eyes that sparkle when he laughs, and his sensual mouth and generous lower lip, and you're probably wondering what woman in her right mind wouldn't want Greg's strong, capable surgeon's hands working their magic on her—kids or no kids!

Personality Traits:
An acclaimed neurosurgeon, Greg Wilder is a celebrity of sorts in the planned community of Woodland, Maryland. Authoritative, debonair, self-confident, his reputation for engaging in one casual relationship after another almost overshadows his prowess as a doctor. In reality, Greg dates more out of necessity than anything else, since he has to attend one social function after another. He considers most of the events boring and wishes he could spend more time with his children. But his profession is a difficult and demanding one—and being both father and mother to four kids isn't any less so. A thoughtful, generous, sometimes befuddled father, Greg tries to do it all. Cerebral, he uses his intellect and skill rather than physical strength to win his victories. However, he never expected to come up against one Mary Magdalene May!

Heroine:
MARY MAGDALENE MAY, called Maggie by her friends, is the thirty-two-year-old mother of three children. She has shoulder-length auburn hair, and green eyes that shout her Irish heritage. With high cheekbones and an upturned nose covered with a smattering of freckles, Maggie thinks of herself more as the girl-next-door type. Certainly, she believes, she could never be one of Greg Wilder's beautiful escorts.

Setting: The small town of Woodland, Maryland

The Story:
Surgeon Greg Wilder wanted to court the feisty and beautiful widow who'd been caring for his four kids, but she just wouldn't let him past her doorstep! Sure that his interest was only casual, and that he preferred more sophisticated women, Maggie May vowed to keep Greg at arm's length. But he wouldn't take no for an answer. And once he'd crashed through her defenses and pulled her into his arms, he was tireless—and reckless—in his campaign to win her over. Maggie had found it tough enough to resist one determined doctor; now he threatened to call in his kids and hers as reinforcements—seven rowdy snags to romance!

Cover scene:
As if romancing Maggie weren't hard enough, Greg can't seem to find time to spend with her without their children around. Stealing a private moment on the stairs in Maggie's house, Greg and Maggie embrace. She is standing one step above him, but she still has to look up at him to see into his eyes. Greg's hands are on her hips, and her hands are resting on his shoulders. Maggie is wearing a very sheer, short pink nightgown, and Greg has on wheat-colored jeans and a navy and yellow striped rugby shirt. Do they have time to kiss?

THE HOMETOWN HUNK CONTEST

IN A CLASS BY ITSELF
(Originally Published as LOVESWEPT #66)
By Sandra Brown

COVER NOTES

The Characters:

Hero:
LOGAN WEBSTER would have no trouble posing for a
Scandinavian travel poster. His wheat-colored hair always
seems to be tousled, defying attempts to control it, and
falls across his wide forehead. Thick eyebrows one shade
darker than his hair accentuate his crystal blue eyes. He
has a slender nose that flairs slightly over a mouth that
testifies to both sensitivity and strength. The faint lines
around his eyes and alongside his mouth give the impression that reaching the ripe age of 30 wasn't all fun and
games for him. Logan's square, determined jaw is punctuated by a vertical cleft. His broad shoulders and narrow
waist add to his tall, lean appearance.

Personality traits:
Logan Webster has had to scrape and save and fight for
everything he's gotten. Born into a poor farm family, he
was driven to succeed and overcome his "wrong side of
the tracks" image. His businesses include cattle, real estate, and natural gas. Now a pillar of the community,
Logan's life has been a true rags-to-riches story. Only
Sandra Brown's own words can describe why he is masculinity epitomized: "Logan had 'the walk,' that saddle-
tramp saunter that was inherent to native Texan men,
passed down through generations of cowboys. It was, without even trying to be, sexy. The unconscious roll of the
hips, the slow strut, the flexed knees, the slouching stance,
the deceptive laziness that hid a latent aggressiveness."
Wow! And not only does he have "the walk," but he's fun

and generous and kind. Even with his wealth, he feels at home living in his small hometown with simple, hard-working, middle-class, backbone-of-America folks. A born leader, people automatically gravitate toward him.

Heroine:
DANI QUINN is a sophisticated twenty-eight-year-old woman. Dainty, her body compact, she is utterly feminine. Dani's pale, lustrous hair is moonlight and honey spun together, and because it is very straight, she usually wears it in a chignon. With golden eyes to match her golden hair, Dani is the one woman Logan hasn't been able to get off his mind for the ten years they've been apart.

Setting: Primarily on Logan's ranch in East Texas.

The Story:
Ten years had passed since Dani Quinn had graduated from high school in the small Texas town, ten years since the night her elopement with Logan Webster had ended in disaster. Now Dani approached her tenth reunion with uncertainty. Logan would be there . . . Logan, the only man who'd ever made her shiver with desire and need, but would she have the courage to face the fury in his eyes? She couldn't defend herself against his anger and hurt—to do so would demand she reveal the secret sorrow she shared with no one. Logan's touch had made her his so long ago. Could he reach past the pain to make her his for all time?

Cover Scene:
It's sunset, and Logan and Dani are standing beside the swimming pool on his ranch, embracing. The pool is surrounded by semitropical plants and lush flower beds. In the distance, acres of rolling pasture land resembling a green lake undulate into dense, piney woods. Dani is wearing a strapless, peacock blue bikini and sandals with leather ties that wrap around her ankles. Her hair is straight and loose, falling to the middle of her back. Logan has on a light-colored pair of corduroy shorts and a short-sleeved designer knit shirt in a pale shade of yellow.

THE HOMETOWN HUNK CONTEST

C.J.'S FATE
(Originally Published as LOVESWEPT #32)
By Kay Hooper

COVER NOTES

The Characters:

Hero:
FATE WESTON easily could have walked straight off an Indian reservation. His raven black hair and strong, well-molded features testify to his heritage. But somewhere along the line genetics threw Fate a curve—his eyes are the deepest, darkest blue imaginable! Above those blue eyes are dark slanted eyebrows, and fanning out from those eyes are faint laugh lines—the only sign of the fact that he's thirty-four years old. Tall, Fate moves with easy, loose-limbed grace. Although he isn't an athlete, Fate takes very good care of himself, and it shows in his strong physique. Striking at first glance and fascinating with each succeeding glance, the serious expressions on his face make him look older than his years, but with one smile he looks boyish again.

Personality traits:
Fate possesses a keen sense of humor. His heavy-lidded, intelligent eyes are capable of concealment, but there is a shrewdness in them that reveals the man hadn't needed college or a law degree to be considered intelligent. The set of his head tells you that he is proud—perhaps even a bit arrogant. He is attractive and perfectly well aware of that fact. Unconventional, paradoxical, tender, silly, lusty, gentle, comical, serious, absurd, and endearing are all words that come to mind when you think of Fate. He is not ashamed to be everything a man can be. A defense attorney by profession, one can detect a bit of frustrated actor in his character. More than anything else, though, it's the

impression of humor about him—reinforced by the elusive dimple in his cheek—that makes Fate Weston a scrumptious hero!

Heroine:
C.J. ADAMS is a twenty-six-year-old research librarian. Unaware of her own attractiveness, C.J. tends to play down her pixylike figure and tawny gold eyes. But once she meets Fate, she no longer feels that her short, burnished copper curls and the sprinkling of freckles on her nose make her unappealing. He brings out the vixen in her, and changes the smart, bookish woman who professed to have no interest in men into the beautiful, sexy woman she really was all along. Now, if only he could get her to tell him what C.J. stands for!

Setting: Ski lodge in Aspen, Colorado

The Story:
C.J. Adams had been teased enough about her seeming lack of interest in the opposite sex. On a ski trip with her five best friends, she impulsively embraced a handsome stranger, pretending they were secret lovers—and the delighted lawyer who joined in her impetuous charade seized the moment to deepen the kiss. Astonished at his reaction, C.J. tried to nip their romance in the bud—but found herself nipping at his neck instead! She had met her match in a man who could answer her witty remarks with clever ripostes of his own, and a lover whose caresses aroused in her a passionate need she'd never suspected that she could feel. Had destiny somehow tossed them together?

Cover Scene:
C.J. and Fate virtually have the ski slopes to themselves early one morning, and they take advantage of it! Frolicking in a snow drift, Fate is covering C.J. with snow—and kisses! They are flushed from the cold weather and from the excitement of being in love. C.J. is wearing a sky-blue, one-piece, tight-fitting ski outfit that zips down the front. Fate is wearing a navy blue parka and matching ski pants.

THE HOMETOWN HUNK CONTEST

THE LADY AND THE UNICORN
(Originally Published as LOVESWEPT #29)
By Iris Johansen

COVER NOTES

The Characters:

Hero:
Not classically handsome, RAFE SANTINE's blunt, craggy
features reinforce the quality of overpowering virility about
him. He has wide, Slavic cheekbones and a bold, thrust-
ing chin, which give the impression of strength and authority. Thick black eyebrows are set over piercing dark
eyes. He wears his heavy, dark hair long. His large frame
measures in at almost six feet four inches, and it's hard to
believe that a man with such brawny shoulders and strong
thighs could exhibit the pantherlike grace which charac-
terizes Rafe's movements. Rafe Santine is definitely a man
to be reckoned with, and heroine Janna Cannon does just
that!

Personality traits:
Our hero is a man who radiates an aura of power and
danger, and women find him intriguing and irresistible.
Rafe Santine is a self-made billionaire at the age of thirty-
eight. Almost entirely self-educated, he left school at sixteen to work on his first construction job, and by the time
he was twenty-three, he owned the company. From there
he branched out into real estate, computers, and oil. Rafe
reportedly changes mistresses as often as he changes shirts.
His reputation for ruthless brilliance has been earned over
years of fighting to the top of the economic ladder from
the slums of New York. His gruff manner and hard personality hide the tender, vulnerable side of him. Rafe also
possesses an insatiable thirst for knowledge that is a
passion with him. Oddly enough, he has a wry sense of

humor that surfaces unexpectedly from time to time. And, though cynical to the extreme, he never lets his natural skepticism interfere with his innate sense of justice.

Heroine:
JANNA CANNON, a game warden for a small wildlife preserve, is a very dedicated lady. She is tall at five feet nine inches and carries herself in a stately way. Her long hair is dark brown and is usually twisted into a single thick braid in back. Of course, Rafe never lets her keep her hair braided when they make love! Janna is one quarter Cherokee Indian by heritage, and she possesses the dark eyes and skin of her ancestors.

Setting: Rafe's estate in Carmel, California

The Story:
Janna Cannon scaled the high walls of Rafe Santine's private estate, afraid of nothing and determined to appeal to the powerful man who could save her beloved animal preserve. She bewitched his guard dogs, then cast a spell of enchantment over him as well. Janna's profound grace, her caring nature, made the tough and proud Rafe grow mercurial in her presence. She offered him a gift he'd never risked reaching out for before—but could he trust his own emotions enough to open himself to her love?

Cover Scene:
In the gazebo overlooking the rugged cliffs at the edge of the Pacific Ocean, Rafe and Janna share a passionate moment together. The gazebo is made of redwood and the interior is small and cozy. Scarlet cushions cover the benches, and matching scarlet curtains hang from the eaves, caught back by tasseled sashes to permit the sea breeze to whip through the enclosure. Rafe is wearing black suede pants and a charcoal gray crew-neck sweater. Janna is wearing a safari-style khaki shirt-and-slacks outfit and suede desert boots. They embrace against the breathtaking backdrop of wild, crashing, white-crested waves pounding the rocks and cliffs below.

THE HOMETOWN HUNK CONTEST

CHARADE
(Originally Published as LOVESWEPT #74)
By Joan Elliott Pickart

COVER NOTES

The Characters:

Hero:
The phrase tall, dark, and handsome was coined to describe TENNES WHITNEY. His coal black hair reaches past his collar in back, and his fathomless steel gray eyes are framed by the kind of thick, dark lashes that a woman would kill to have. Darkly tanned, Tennes has a straight nose and a square chin, with—you guessed it!—a Kirk Douglas cleft. Tennes oozes masculinity and virility. He's a handsome son-of-a-gun!

Personality traits:
A shrewd, ruthless business tycoon, Tennes is a man of strength and principle. He's perfected the art of buying floundering companies and turning them around financially, then selling them at a profit. He possesses a sixth sense about business—in short, he's a winner! But there are two sides to his personality. Always in cool command, Tennes, who fears no man or challenge, is rendered emotionally vulnerable when faced with his elderly aunt's illness. His deep devotion to the woman who raised him clearly casts him as a warm, compassionate guy—not at all like the tough-as-nails executive image he presents. Leave it to heroine Whitney Jordan to discover the real man behind the complicated enigma.

Heroine:
WHITNEY JORDAN's russet-colored hair floats past her shoulders in glorious waves. Her emerald green eyes, full breasts, and long, slender legs—not to mention her peaches-

and-cream complexion—make her eye-poppingly attractive. How can Tennes resist the twenty-six-year-old beauty? And how can Whitney consider becoming serious with him? If their romance flourishes, she may end up being Whitney Whitney!

Setting: Los Angeles, California

The Story:
One moment writer Whitney Jordan was strolling the aisles of McNeil's Department Store, plotting the untimely demise of a soap opera heartthrob; the next, she was nearly knocked over by a real-life stunner who implored her to be his fiancée! The ailing little gray-haired aunt who'd raised him had one final wish, he said—to see her dear nephew Tennes married to the wonderful girl he'd described in his letters . . . only that girl hadn't existed—until now! Tennes promised the masquerade would last only through lunch, but Whitney gave such an inspired performance that Aunt Olive refused to let her go. And what began as a playful romantic deception grew more breathlessly real by the minute. . . .

Cover Scene:
Whitney's living room is bright and cheerful. The gray carpeting and blue sofa with green and blue throw pillows gives the apartment a cool but welcoming appearance. Sitting on the sofa next to Tennes, Whitney is wearing a black crepe dress that is simply cut but stunning. It is cut low over her breasts and held at the shoulders by thin straps. The skirt falls to her knees in soft folds and the bodice is nipped in at the waist with a matching belt. She has on black high heels, but prefers not to wear any jewelry to spoil the simplicity of the dress. Tennes is dressed in a black suit with a white silk shirt and a deep red tie.

THE HOMETOWN HUNK CONTEST

FOR THE LOVE OF SAMI
(Originally Published as LOVESWEPT #34)
By Fayrene Preston

COVER NOTES

Hero:
DANIEL PARKER-ST. JAMES is every woman's dream come true. With glossy black hair and warm, reassuring blue eyes, he makes our heroine melt with just a glance. Daniel's lean face is chiseled into assertive planes. His lips are full and firmly sculptured, and his chin has the determined and arrogant thrust to it only a man who's sure of himself can carry off. Daniel has a lot in common with Clark Kent. Both wear glasses, and when Daniel removes them to make love to Sami, she thinks he really is Superman!

Personality traits:
Daniel Parker-St. James is one of the Twin Cities' most respected attorneys. He's always in the news, either in the society columns with his latest society lady, or on the front page with his headline cases. He's brilliant and takes on only the toughest cases—usually those that involve millions of dollars. Daniel has a reputation for being a deadly opponent in the courtroom. Because he's from a socially prominent family and is a Harvard graduate, it's expected that he'll run for the Senate one day. Distinguished-looking and always distinctively dressed—he's fastidious about his appearance—Daniel gives off an unassailable air of authority and absolute control.

Heroine:
SAMUELINA (SAMI) ADKINSON is secretly a wealthy heiress. No one would guess. She lives in a converted warehouse loft, dresses to suit no one but herself, and dabbles in the creative arts. Sami is twenty-six years old, with

long, honey-colored hair. She wears soft, wispy bangs and has very thick brown lashes framing her golden eyes. Of medium height, Sami has to look up to gaze into Daniel's deep blue eyes.

Setting: St. Paul, Minnesota

The Story:
Unpredictable heiress Sami Adkinson had endeared herself to the most surprising people—from the bag ladies in the park she protected . . . to the mobster who appointed himself her guardian . . . to her exasperated but loving friends. Then Sami was arrested while demonstrating to save baby seals, and it took powerful attorney Daniel Parker-St. James to bail her out. Daniel was smitten, soon cherishing Sami and protecting her from her night fears. Sami reveled in his love—and resisted it too. And holding on to Sami, Daniel discovered, was like trying to hug quicksilver. . . .

Cover Scene:
The interior of Daniel's house is very grand and supremely formal, the decor sophisticated, refined, and quietly tasteful, just like Daniel himself. Rich traditional fabrics cover plush oversized custom sofas and Regency wing chairs. Queen Anne furniture is mixed with Chippendale and is subtly complemented with Oriental accent pieces. In the library, floor-to-ceiling bookcases filled with rare books provide the backdrop for Sami and Daniel's embrace. Sami is wearing a gold satin sheath gown. The dress has a high neckline, but in back is cut provocatively to the waist. Her jewels are exquisite. The necklace is made up of clusters of flowers created by large, flawless diamonds. From every cluster a huge, perfectly matched teardrop emerald hangs. The earrings are composed of an even larger flower cluster, and an equally huge teardrop-shaped emerald hangs from each one. Daniel is wearing a classic, elegant tuxedo.

LOVESWEPT® HOMETOWN HUNK CONTEST

OFFICIAL RULES

> IN A CLASS BY ITSELF by Sandra Brown
> FOR THE LOVE OF SAMI by Fayrene Preston
> C.J.'S FATE by Kay Hooper
> THE LADY AND THE UNICORN by Iris Johansen
> CHARADE by Joan Elliott Pickart
> DARLING OBSTACLES by Barbara Boswell

1. NO PURCHASE NECESSARY. Enter the HOMETOWN HUNK contest by completing the Official Entry Form below and enclosing a sharp color full-length photograph (easy to see details, with the photo being no smaller than 2½" × 3½") of the man you think perfectly represents one of the heroes from the above-listed books which are described in the accompanying Loveswept cover notes. Please be sure to fill out the Official Entry Form completely, and also be sure to clearly print on the back of the man's photograph the man's name, address, city, state, zip code, telephone number, date of birth, your name, address, city, state, zip code, telephone number, your relationship, if any, to the man (e.g. wife, girlfriend) as well as the title of the Loveswept book for which you are entering the man. If you do not have an Official Entry Form, you can print all of the required information on a 3" × 5" card and attach it to the photograph with all the necessary information printed on the back of the photograph as well. YOUR HERO MUST SIGN BOTH THE BACK OF THE OFFICIAL ENTRY FORM (OR 3" × 5" CARD) AND THE PHOTOGRAPH TO SIGNIFY HIS CONSENT TO BEING ENTERED IN THE CONTEST. Completed entries should be sent to:

> BANTAM BOOKS
> HOMETOWN HUNK CONTEST
> Department CN
> 666 Fifth Avenue
> New York, New York 10102–0023

All photographs and entries become the property of Bantam Books and will not be returned under any circumstances.

2. Six men will be chosen by the Loveswept authors as a HOMETOWN HUNK (one HUNK per Loveswept title). By entering the contest, each winner and each person who enters a winner agrees to abide by Bantam Books' rules and to be subject to Bantam Books' eligibility requirements. Each winning HUNK and each person who enters a winner will be required to sign all papers deemed necessary by Bantam Books before receiving any prize. Each winning HUNK will be flown via **United Airlines** from his closest United Airlines-serviced city to New York City and will stay at the ⋅⋅⋅ SUSSE͟X Hotel—the ideal hotel for business or pleasure in midtown Manhattan—for two nights. Winning HUNKS' meals and hotel transfers will be provided by Bantam Books. Travel and hotel arrangements are made by *RELIABLE TRAVEL INTERNATIONAL* and are subject to availability and to Bantam Books' date requirements. Each winning HUNK will pose with a female model at a photographer's studio for a photograph that will serve as the basis of a Loveswept front cover. Each winning HUNK will receive a $150.00 modeling fee. Each winning HUNK will be required to sign an Affidavit of Eligibility and Model's Release supplied by Bantam Books. (Approximate retail value of HOMETOWN HUNK'S PRIZE: $900.00). The six people who send in a winning HOMETOWN HUNK photograph that is used by Bantam will receive free for one year each, LOVESWEPT romance paperback books published by Bantam during that year. (Approximate retail value: $180.00.) Each person who submits a winning photograph

will also be required to sign an Affidavit of Eligibility and Promotional Release supplied by Bantam Books. All winning HUNKS' (as well as the people who submit the winning photographs) names, addresses, biographical data and likenesses may be used by Bantam Books for publicity and promotional purposes without any additional compensation. There will be no prize substitutions or cash equivalents made.

3. All completed entries must be received by Bantam Books no later than September 15, 1988. Bantam Books is not responsible for lost or misdirected entries. The finalists will be selected by Loveswept editors and the six winning HOMETOWN HUNKS will be selected by the six authors of the participating Loveswept books. Winners will be selected on the basis of how closely the judges believe they reflect the descriptions of the books' heroes. Winners will be notified on or about October 31, 1988. If there are insufficient entries or if in the judges' opinions, no entry is suitable or adequately reflects the descriptions of the hero(s) in the book(s), Bantam may decide not to award a prize for the applicable book(s) and may reissue the book(s) at its discretion.

4. The contest is open to residents of the U.S. and Canada, except the Province of Quebec, and is void where prohibited by law. All federal and local regulations apply. Employees of Reliable Travel International, Inc., United Airlines, the Summit Hotel, and the Bantam Doubleday Dell Publishing Group, Inc., their subsidiaries and affiliates, and their immediate families are ineligible to enter.

5. For an extra copy of the Official Rules, the Official Entry Form, and the accompanying Loveswept cover notes, send your request and a self-addressed stamped envelope (Vermont and Washington State residents need not affix postage) before August 20, 1988 to the address listed in Paragraph 1 above.

LOVESWEPT® HOMETOWN HUNK OFFICIAL ENTRY FORM

BANTAM BOOKS
HOMETOWN HUNK CONTEST
Dept. CN
666 Fifth Avenue
New York, New York 10102–0023

HOMETOWN HUNK CONTEST

YOUR NAME_____

YOUR ADDRESS_____

CITY_____ STATE_____ ZIP_____

THE NAME OF THE LOVESWEPT BOOK FOR WHICH YOU ARE ENTERING THIS PHOTO

_____by_____

YOUR RELATIONSHIP TO YOUR HERO_____

YOUR HERO'S NAME_____

YOUR HERO'S ADDRESS_____

CITY_____ STATE_____ ZIP_____

YOUR HERO'S TELEPHONE #_____

YOUR HERO'S DATE OF BIRTH_____

YOUR HERO'S SIGNATURE CONSENTING TO HIS PHOTOGRAPH ENTRY

_____